CRESSIDA BLYTHEWOOD

The Lady's Scandalous Game

Copyright © 2024 by Cressida Blythewood

All rights reserved. No part of this publication may be reproduced, stored or transmitted in any form or by any means, electronic, mechanical, photocopying, recording, scanning, or otherwise without written permission from the publisher. It is illegal to copy this book, post it to a website, or distribute it by any other means without permission.

This novel is entirely a work of fiction. The names, characters and incidents portrayed in it are the work of the author's imagination. Any resemblance to actual persons, living or dead, events or localities is entirely coincidental.

First edition

This book was professionally typeset on Reedsy.
Find out more at reedsy.com

Contents

1	A Glittering Assembly	1
2	The Scandalous Announcement	4
3	The Society's Games	10
4	The Aftermath	14
5	Whispers in the Drawing Rooms	18
6	A Gossip's Delight	23
7	An Unfortunate Encounter	28
8	The First Signs	33
9	A Society in Suspense	38
10	The Symptoms Escalate	43
11	A Passionate Picnic	47
12	The Rumor's Reach	52
13	The Uncomfortable Truth	58
14	Confessions and Revelations	62
15	The Unveiling Truth	67
16	Cassian Cavendish	72
17	The Mask of Innocence	78
18	A Chance Encounter	84
19	A Delicate Balance	90
20	The Pressure Mounts	95
21	A Tense Dinner Party	100
22	An Unexpected Meeting	105
23	Conflicted Hearts	110
24	The Unveiling	115
25	The Bitter Honesty	119
26	The Weight of Reality	124

27	The Grand Ball	129
28	Cassian's Realization	134
29	A Serious Proposal	142
30	The Pact	147
31	A Sister's Dilemma	151
32	A Heartfelt Decision	156
33	Stepping Into the Light	161
34	The Courage	166
35	The Plan Unfolds	170
36	A Night to Remember	173
37	A Joyous Celebration	178
38	Love Making	183
39	The Sweet and Unexpected	187
40	A Greetings from Future Love	193
41	A Promise for the Future	198
About the Author		203
Also by Cressida Blythewood		204

1

A Glittering Assembly

If there is one thing I've learned about high society, it's that the higher you climb, the more precarious your position becomes—especially when one is perched on the societal ladder with a name like Fairchild, which, though respectable, is hardly the sort of thing that inspires hushed awe or desperate curtsies. But alas, being a Fairchild comes with its own set of challenges, such as enduring endless invitations to salons hosted by women who have mastered the art of idle gossip and lethal smiles.

And so, I found myself at the salon of Lady Evelyn, the Duchess of Abernathy—a woman who could probably organize a revolution over tea and still have time to critique the fashion choices of her guests. The room was a glittering spectacle of lace, silk, and feathers, with every lady and gentleman present determined to outdo the other in sartorial excess. I had opted for a gown of pale blue muslin, elegant enough to be noticed but not so ostentatious as to attract Lady Evelyn's eagle eye. I wasn't about to give her any more ammunition than she already had.

I made my way through the throng, offering the appropriate nods and smiles, each one practiced to perfection. The art of appearing both interested and aloof was something I had honed over many years, much like a soldier polishing his saber before battle. And believe me, these gatherings were a battlefield—one where a single misstep could mean social ruin, or worse, a marriage proposal from the likes of Lord Fotheringay, who was currently ogling the pastries with a hunger that was frankly alarming.

"Isabella, darling!" Lady Beatrice Whitford, my dearest and most meddlesome friend, appeared at my side, her eyes sparkling with mischief. Beatrice was the kind of woman who could find trouble in an empty room and then drag you into it, all while looking perfectly innocent. Today, her mischief was directed at the gathering of gentlemen who had formed a loose circle around Lady Evelyn's chaise longue, clearly hoping to win her favor—or, more likely, a place in her will.

"Beatrice, whatever it is you're planning, I am not interested," I said with a raised brow, though the truth was I was more than a little curious. Beatrice had a way of making even the dullest events into something worth attending.

"Oh, but you will be interested, my dear Isabella," she replied, linking her arm with mine and steering me towards the gentlemen. "Lady Evelyn has devised a new game for us—something called 'Forfeits.' It promises to be quite… entertaining."

I narrowed my eyes at her, suspecting that her definition of "entertaining" and mine were worlds apart. "Forfeits? That sounds suspiciously like something that involves embarrassment and public humiliation."

"Precisely," Beatrice said with a grin. "And who better to endure it than us?"

Before I could protest further, we were upon the group, and Lady Evelyn herself was beckoning us closer. Her sharp eyes gleamed with an anticipation that set my nerves on edge. I should have known that nothing good could come from a woman who once staged an entire dinner party as a reenactment of the Battle of Waterloo, complete with miniature cannons and guests assigned the roles of soldiers.

"Ah, Lady Isabella, how delightful that you could join us," Lady Evelyn purred, her voice smooth as silk but with an undercurrent that suggested she had already planned my downfall. "We were just about to begin a game of Forfeits. I do hope you'll play along."

There was no polite way to refuse without causing a scene, and causing a scene at Lady Evelyn's salon was tantamount to social suicide. So, with a smile that I hoped did not resemble a grimace, I agreed.

"What a marvelous idea," I said, my voice bright as a bell. "I do love a good game."

And that was the moment I should have known that my life was about to take a most unexpected turn. But like a fool, I thought I could handle whatever Lady Evelyn had in store. After all, how bad could a little parlor game be?

Little did I know, by the end of the evening, I would find myself embroiled in a scandal so outrageous that even Lady Evelyn herself could not have predicted the outcome.

But I'm getting ahead of myself. First, there was the matter of losing a round of Forfeits, and as it turned out, I was rather spectacular at losing.

2

The Scandalous Announcement

The room fell silent as Lady Evelyn, with the grace of a predator about to pounce, rose from her chaise longue. She surveyed the gathered throng with an expression that could only be described as predatory amusement. I half-expected her to produce a hunting horn and declare open season on anyone unfortunate enough to cross her path.

"Ladies and gentlemen," she began, her voice smooth as buttered silk, "it is time for a little amusement. I trust you are all familiar with the game of Forfeits?"

There were murmurs of agreement, though I noticed a few nervous glances exchanged among the less seasoned guests. Clearly, they had not yet experienced the particular brand of entertainment that Lady Evelyn was known for. The more experienced among us—myself included—knew better than to let our guard down.

"For those who may be unacquainted," Lady Evelyn continued, "the rules are quite simple. Each of you will be required to complete a challenge, and should you fail, you must pay a forfeit. These forfeits can be anything from a recitation of poetry to something more... scandalous." She paused, allowing the implications to settle over the room like a thick fog. "I trust we are all in good spirits this evening, yes?"

There was a general murmur of assent, though I could see the tension in the eyes of some of the guests—no one wanted to be the first to stumble. For my part, I was determined to approach the game with a mixture of caution and cunning. After all, one did not survive in London society without learning how to navigate the treacherous waters of public humiliation.

"Very well," Lady Evelyn said, a smile curving her lips as if she were about to devour us all. "Shall we begin?"

The first challenge was issued to Lord Fotheringay, who was tasked with composing an impromptu verse extolling the virtues of a lemon tart. To his credit, he managed to string together a few rhyming lines that were passable enough, though the tart he praised with such enthusiasm was, in reality, as dry as his wit.

Next came Lady Penelope, who had to describe her most embarrassing childhood memory—a story involving a goose, a bonnet, and a rather unfortunate misunderstanding at a village fair. The tale was met with laughter, though I suspected Lady Penelope's dignity might never fully recover.

As the game progressed, the challenges grew increasingly difficult—and the forfeits more inventive. One gentleman was made to recite Shakespeare while balancing a teacup on his head, while another lady was required to sing an operatic aria in Italian, despite her only knowledge of the language being limited to ordering gelato.

When my turn finally came, I was feeling rather smug. So far, I had managed to avoid any serious pitfalls, and I was confident that whatever challenge Lady Evelyn threw my way, I could handle it with the same aplomb I used to navigate the ton's endless rounds of gossip.

"Lady Isabella," Lady Evelyn purred, her eyes gleaming with something that looked suspiciously like mischief. "Your challenge is to..."

I held my breath, waiting for the inevitable.

"...tell us the most scandalous secret you know."

The room went still. I could feel the weight of a dozen pairs of eyes on me, waiting to see how I would respond. I allowed myself a moment of contemplation, my mind racing through the possibilities. Should I reveal some minor indiscretion I had overheard at a recent ball? Or perhaps invent a harmless rumor that would amuse without causing too much damage?

But then I caught sight of Lady Evelyn's expression—she was expecting me to falter, to stumble, to fail. And something inside me rebelled at the thought of giving her that satisfaction.

"Very well," I said, my voice steady, though my heart was pounding. "I shall tell you a secret."

I let the silence stretch out, watching as the anticipation in the room grew. Lady Evelyn leaned forward ever so slightly, clearly intrigued.

"The most scandalous secret I know," I continued, "is that I have, on occasion, taken tea with a certain gentleman—alone."

There were gasps, and I could practically see the wheels turning in everyone's minds, trying to figure out who this mysterious gentleman could be. Of course, I hadn't actually specified that the gentleman in question. Only I know who that person is and I will never tell. Especially about what we did... more than just having tea together.

Lady Evelyn's eyes narrowed, but she couldn't deny that I had completed the challenge. The game moved on, though I noticed several ladies whispering to each other, clearly speculating about my "scandalous" secret. I allowed myself a small, satisfied smile—so far, so good.

But my satisfaction was short-lived. As the game wore on, I became aware of a growing sense of unease, like an itch just beneath the skin that you can't quite scratch. It wasn't just the palpable tension in the room—though there was plenty of that, too, with every guest eyeing the others like cats in a drawing room full of canaries. No, it was something more insidious, creeping up on me like a bad penny.

As Lady Evelyn called out the challenges one by one, I felt a strange tightness in my chest. It was as if the very air had thickened, the weight of expectation pressing down on my shoulders. I was no stranger to pressure—being a Fairchild practically required it as part of our upbringing—but this was different. My palms were clammy, a delicate sheen of sweat forming despite the coolness of the room. My head began to ache, a dull throb that pulsed in time with the rapid beat of my heart.

I tried to tell myself it was just the evening's excitement—the strain of maintaining my polished facade among such a glittering, and often vicious, crowd. But deep down, I knew something wasn't quite right. I could feel it in my bones, a nagging sensation that something was about to go terribly, dreadfully wrong.

And then it happened.

In the next round, I was dealt a challenge that seemed deceptively simple—a harmless riddle. Under normal circumstances, I would have solved it in a heartbeat, with a flourish and perhaps even a clever retort for good measure. But tonight, fate had other plans.

The moment I opened my mouth to give the answer, the words seemed to stick in my throat, as if they were suddenly made of lead. I could feel the expectant gazes of the other guests, their curiosity tinged with the hope that I might falter. My vision blurred, the edges of the room becoming soft and indistinct, and I had to grip the edge of my chair to steady myself, the cool wood biting into my palms.

Lady Evelyn's eyes bore into mine, a gleam of triumph lighting up her expression. It was as if she had been waiting for this exact moment, her gaze as sharp as a hawk's. She had finally caught me off guard, and I could see the satisfaction curling at the corners of her lips. There was no way I could wriggle out of this one—no clever turn of phrase, no graceful sidestep would save me now.

"Lady Isabella," Lady Evelyn's voice cut through the silence, smooth and deadly as a blade. "It appears you have failed to answer the riddle. You know what that means, don't you?"

I swallowed hard, the enormity of the situation sinking in like a stone. Of course, I knew what it meant. In the twisted world of Lady Evelyn's parlor games, failure was not an option—or rather, it was an option that came with consequences, the kind that society's brightest minds would be discussing over breakfast tomorrow.

I had to pay a forfeit.

And in Lady Evelyn's salon, a forfeit was never just a simple penalty. No, it was a spectacle—a show meant to entertain and, more often than not, embarrass the unlucky participant. I had seen men of stature reduced to singing nursery rhymes in falsetto, and women forced to confess their most humiliating secrets, all in the name of "amusement." And now it was my turn to face the proverbial firing squad.

Lady Evelyn leaned back in her chair, clearly savoring the moment. "Your forfeit," she announced, her voice carrying a note of finality that sent a chill down my spine, "is to create a scandal. Something that will have all of London talking."

The room erupted in a chorus of gasps and murmurs, the shockwaves of her words rippling through the crowd like a stone cast into a still pond. My stomach dropped, and I felt as though the ground had been pulled out from under me. Create a scandal? That was easier said than done. I had spent my entire life avoiding scandal, navigating the treacherous waters of society with care and precision. And now she was asking me to do the very thing I had always avoided.

But there was no way out. The rules of the game were ironclad, and I had accepted the challenge. Now, I had to follow through.

"Very well," I said, my voice surprisingly steady despite the turmoil raging inside me. "I shall create a scandal."

Lady Evelyn smiled, a cat with a canary firmly in its grasp. "Splendid. And to ensure it is truly scandalous, the scandal must be exceptional…"

I nodded and smiled. "I hope you are not disappointed, my Lady."

"I'm waiting…"

As I stood there, the weight of the room's collective gaze pressing down on me, I took a deep breath and allowed myself a moment to gather my thoughts. This was no time to falter. If I was going to navigate the treacherous waters Lady Evelyn had thrown me into, I needed to do so with the grace and poise that society had come to expect from a Fairchild. I had been trained for this—trained to smile when I wanted to scream, to charm when I wanted to flee, to turn the impossible into something manageable.

After all, hadn't I survived countless dinner parties where the wrong word could lead to social ruin? Hadn't I deftly deflected the advances of Lord Hastings without so much as ruffling his overgrown feathers? This was just another test, another performance in the endless play that was life in London's high society. And if there was one thing I knew how to do, it was put on a show.

A plan began to form in my mind, a way to turn this potential disaster into an opportunity. If Lady Evelyn wanted a scandal, then a scandal she would get—but it would be on my terms. I would turn this dare into a spectacle so grand, so audacious, that it would leave the assembled guests talking for weeks. And when they spoke of it, they would do so with admiration, not derision. I would not be the victim of this forfeit; I would be its master.

I could almost hear my mother's voice in my head, reminding me of the importance of poise, of maintaining control even when it seemed all was lost. With that thought in mind, I straightened my spine and allowed a serene smile to settle on my lips.

I would make them believe. And then, I would make them laugh.

With a flourish that would have made an actress on Drury Lane proud, I stepped forward, my gown swirling around my feet like a cloud of pale blue mist. The room, already hushed in anticipation, seemed to hold its breath as I prepared to speak.

"Ladies and gentlemen," I began, my voice carrying across the room, "I have an announcement to make...."

I paused, allowing the suspense to build. I could feel their eyes on me, could sense the curiosity, the eagerness for the scandal they were certain was about to unfold. I let them wait a moment longer—after all, timing was everything.

"I am..." I took another deep breath, as if preparing to reveal a monumental truth, and then, with a dramatic sigh, I said, "expecting."

And so, I embarked on the most audacious lie of my life. Little did I know that the truth would soon catch up with me in ways I never could have imagined.

But that, as they say, is another story.

3

The Society's Games

As I made the announcement, the room fell silent. It was as if time itself had frozen, the air thick with the weight of my words. Every eye was on me, wide and unblinking, every mouth slightly agape. Lady Penelope, ever the embodiment of decorum, actually dropped her fan, the delicate lace and ivory clattering against the floor in a moment of utter shock. The silence stretched on, and I could feel the collective breath of the room being held, as if they were waiting for the punchline to a joke they weren't sure they wanted to hear.

And then, like a dam breaking, the laughter began. It started hesitantly, a few nervous titters that quickly grew into full-bodied mirth, rippling through the room until it echoed off the walls. The sound was almost a relief, as though the tension had been lifted in one great exhale. They thought it was a joke—a clever, audacious prank delivered with the kind of wit they had come to expect from me. Who was I to disabuse them of that notion?

I allowed myself a small, amused laugh, as if sharing in their jest, and offered a playful wink to the nearest group of ladies. "Why, you didn't think I was serious, did you?" I said, my tone light and teasing. "I simply couldn't resist the opportunity to keep you all on your toes."

The laughter grew louder, now tinged with admiration. I could see it in their eyes—relief, certainly, but also a newfound respect for my audacity. The men exchanged knowing glances, while the women hid their smiles behind their fans, clearly impressed by my daring. It wasn't every day that someone managed to pull off such a scandalous stunt with such grace.

"Isabella, you wicked creature," Lady Beatrice said as she sidled up to me, her eyes sparkling with mirth. She was my closest friend, and her approval meant more to me than I cared to admit. "You nearly gave poor Lady Penelope a fit."

I turned to Lady Penelope, who was still recovering from the shock, her cheeks flushed a deep pink. "I do apologize, Penelope," I said with a grin, though my apology was more for show than sincerity. After all, what was a little lighthearted scandal among friends?

Lady Penelope waved her hand dismissively, though her eyes still held a trace of bewilderment. "Oh, you had us all fooled, Isabella. For a moment, I actually believed you."

"That was the idea," I said with a laugh, playing up the role of the mischievous trickster. "A little fun to liven up the evening."

And liven it up, I had. The room, which had been stifling with tension just moments before, was now buzzing with excitement. The earlier unease had melted away, replaced by a sense of camaraderie, as if we had all been in on the joke together. It was as though the scandal Lady Evelyn had sought to orchestrate had been defused, turned into a source of entertainment instead.

"But you were magnificent, Isabella. I don't think anyone expected you to carry out that dare with such... flair!" she chuckled.

I chuckled, though the sound was tinged with the lingering tension I had yet to fully shake. "It was either that or admit defeat, and you know how much I loathe losing."

"Indeed," Beatrice said with a small laugh. She leaned in closer, her voice lowering to a conspiratorial whisper. "You're sure there's no truth to it, right? No surprise announcements in the future?"

I rolled my eyes with a chuckle, reassuring her with a playful nudge. "Beatrice, please. There's no baby in this belly, I assure you. It was just a ruse, a bit of fun at Lady Evelyn's expense."

She nodded, a smile still tugging at her lips, though I could see the faintest trace of concern lingering in her eyes. "You know how these things can spiral,

Isabella. Just be careful."

I squeezed her hand gently. "I will, Bea. I've got this under control."

But as I looked around the room, I caught Lady Evelyn's eye. To my surprise, she wasn't scowling or fuming as I might have expected. Instead, there was a glint of something almost like approval in her gaze. She inclined her head ever so slightly, a silent acknowledgment that I had, indeed, passed her test. The smugness in her expression had faded, replaced by a grudging respect.

"Bravo, Lady Isabella," she said, her voice carrying just enough to be heard by those nearest to her. "You have truly outdone yourself tonight."

I offered a graceful curtsey in response, accepting her praise with the same poise I had maintained throughout the evening. But I couldn't help but notice the hint of defeat in her eyes, as if she realized that her attempt to unsettle me had backfired spectacularly. The game had been played, and I had won.

Or so I thought.

As the evening continued, the guests congratulated me on my performance, their laughter and admiration a balm to my frayed nerves. Lady Beatrice remained by my side, occasionally casting me an amused, albeit slightly wary, glance. "Well, if nothing else, you've certainly given them something to talk about," she remarked, her tone light but with an edge of caution.

I smiled at her, though the weight of her words lingered in the back of my mind. "Yes, I suppose I have."

But even as I smiled and joked with the other guests, accepting their compliments with practiced ease, I couldn't shake the feeling that something had shifted. The seed of the rumor had been planted, and though the room had erupted in laughter tonight, I knew that by morning, there would be whispers. Whispers that might take on a life of their own, twisting and turning until the truth was no longer recognizable.

But for now, I pushed those thoughts aside. Tonight, I had turned what could have been a disaster into a triumph, and that was enough.

Or so I hoped.

As the evening drew to a close, I found myself alone for a moment, the remnants of laughter still echoing in my ears. I glanced down at my still-flat stomach, a wry smile tugging at my lips. I had reassured Beatrice that there was no truth to the rumors, but a small, insistent voice in the back of my mind reminded me that life had a way of surprising even the most careful of planners.

I took a deep breath, squaring my shoulders. That's not likely to happen. If I was pregnant then I would have realized it. Moreover, our last meeting was a few weeks ago before he left for Birmingham. But, whatever the future held, I would face it with the same wit and audacity that had carried me through tonight. After all, I was Isabella Fairchild—scandals might come and go, but I would always remain one step ahead.

As I rejoined the party, the smiles and laughter of the guests surrounding me, I couldn't help but feel a surge of pride. I had played the game, and for now, I had won. But as I caught Lady Evelyn's eye once more, I couldn't help but wonder what the next move in this unspoken game would be.

And as the night drew to a close, with the whispers of tomorrow already beginning to form, I knew that this was only the beginning. The scandal of the season had been born, and with it, the promise of more surprises yet to come.

4

The Aftermath

As the evening's revelry finally began to wind down, I found myself standing by one of Lady Evelyn's grand windows, gazing out at the darkened streets of London. The flickering gas lamps cast long, wavering shadows on the cobblestones, and the distant clatter of horse-drawn carriages echoed faintly through the cool night air. It was a quiet moment, a brief respite after the whirlwind of the evening's events, and I welcomed the chance to gather my thoughts.

Behind me, the last of the guests were taking their leave, offering final compliments to Lady Evelyn and exchanging knowing smiles as they made their way to the door. The air was still thick with the remnants of laughter and the clinking of glasses, but the energy in the room had shifted, mellowed by the lateness of the hour.

"Isabella," came a familiar voice, soft and warm, "there you are."

I turned to find Lady Beatrice approaching, her expression a mix of fondness and concern. She had shed her earlier mischievous grin and now looked at me with the kind of serious, attentive gaze that only a true friend could offer. Her honey-blonde curls framed her face, and she had draped a delicate shawl over her shoulders, warding off the evening chill.

"Beatrice," I replied, smiling as she joined me by the window. "I was just taking a moment to breathe. It's been quite the evening, hasn't it?"

"That it has," she agreed, her tone light but carrying an undertone of seriousness.

I glanced at her, catching the hint of worry in her eyes. "You're still concerned about the consequences, are you?"

Beatrice hesitated, her gaze drifting to the floor before meeting mine again. "I am, a little. I know it was all in good fun, but you did make quite the statement tonight. Rumors have a way of growing, even when they start as jokes."

I waved a hand dismissively, determined not to let her concern dampen my spirits. "Oh, Beatrice, don't worry so much. By tomorrow morning, everyone will have moved on to the next piece of gossip. Lady Evelyn will surely stage another grand spectacle soon enough, and my little performance will be all but forgotten."

Beatrice didn't look entirely convinced, but she nodded nonetheless. "Perhaps you're right. Still, I can't help but think there's something more to this. You know how society is, Isabella—once a rumor takes root, it's nearly impossible to stop it from spreading."

I sighed, understanding her point but unwilling to dwell on it. "True, but honestly, what's the worst that could happen? People will laugh, and then they'll realize it was all a bit of fun. They'll remember tonight as one of Lady Evelyn's more entertaining gatherings, and that will be that."

Beatrice studied me for a moment, her blue eyes searching mine as if looking for any sign of doubt. Finding none, she sighed and offered a small smile. "You're probably right. I suppose I'm just being overly cautious."

"Which is why I value your friendship so much," I said, nudging her playfully with my elbow. "You keep me grounded, even when I'm floating off into the clouds of my own making."

Beatrice chuckled, her worry easing slightly. "Well, someone has to keep you in check. Otherwise, who knows what kind of trouble you'd get into?"

"Oh, I'm sure I'd manage just fine," I teased, though in truth, I was grateful for her presence. Beatrice had always been the voice of reason in our friendship, the one who could see potential pitfalls long before I even noticed there was a road ahead. She had saved me from more than a few social missteps over the years, and I trusted her instincts implicitly.

We stood in companionable silence for a few moments, watching as the last of the guests departed, their laughter fading into the night. The grand salon, which had been so full of life and energy just moments ago, now seemed almost serene, the remnants of the evening's festivities lying scattered across the room like the aftermath of a summer storm.

"Do you ever wonder," Beatrice mused quietly, "what it would be like to live a life without all of this?" She gestured vaguely to the grand room around us, her eyes distant. "Without the constant scrutiny, the need to maintain appearances, the endless games we play just to stay afloat?"

I glanced at her, surprised by the sudden shift in conversation. "What do you mean?"

Beatrice sighed, her shoulders slumping slightly. "I mean... do you ever wish we could just be ourselves, without worrying about what everyone else thinks? That we could live our lives freely, without the weight of society's expectations pressing down on us?"

I considered her words, my thoughts drifting back to the evening's events. It was a fair question—one that had crossed my mind more than once, especially on nights like this, when the pressure to perform felt almost suffocating. But even as the idea of a simpler, freer life appealed to me, I knew that it was a fantasy, one that could never truly be realized within the confines of our world.

"Sometimes," I admitted softly. "But I also know that this is the life we were born into. And for all its flaws and frustrations, it's the only life we know. We can't just walk away from it."

"No," Beatrice agreed, though there was a wistfulness in her voice. "I suppose we can't. But it doesn't stop me from wishing, sometimes."

I reached out and squeezed her hand, offering what comfort I could. "We may not be able to change the world, Beatrice, but we can choose how we navigate it. And tonight, I chose to have a little fun. Who knows? Maybe I'll even inspire others to take themselves a little less seriously."

Beatrice smiled, though it was tinged with sadness. "Perhaps. But just promise me one thing, Isabella."

"Anything."

"If this rumor starts to grow… if it becomes something more than just a joke… promise me you'll be careful. I don't want to see you get hurt."

I squeezed her hand again, touched by her concern. "I promise, Beatrice. But truly, I don't think it will come to that. By this time tomorrow, I'll be just another lady who told a cheeky joke at a party, and nothing more."

She nodded, though the worry didn't entirely leave her eyes. "I hope you're right."

With that, we let the conversation drift into more lighthearted topics, discussing the latest fashions, the most recent scandal involving Lord Fotheringay's unfortunate run-in with a tray of éclairs, and whether Lady Penelope's new hairstyle would become the talk of the ton.

But as we laughed and chatted, a small voice at the back of my mind whispered that perhaps Beatrice was right to be concerned. Perhaps there was more to this night than just a harmless jest. But I pushed the thought aside, refusing to let it take root.

After all, I had won the game tonight. I had outmaneuvered Lady Evelyn, entertained the guests, and maintained my composure in the face of a daunting challenge. What more could society possibly throw at me?

As Beatrice and I finally said our goodbyes and made our way out into the cool night air, I felt a sense of relief wash over me. The evening was over, and tomorrow would be a new day—a day in which, I was certain, this evening's events would fade into the background, just another story in the endless tapestry of London's social scene.

Little did I know, the real story was only just beginning.

And as the night closed in around us, I couldn't shake the feeling that I was standing on the edge of something far greater, far more dangerous, than I had ever anticipated.

But for now, I would let the night carry me home, confident that I had faced the evening's challenges with grace and wit, and that tomorrow would be just another ordinary day in the life of Lady Isabella Fairchild.

How wrong I was.

5

Whispers in the Drawing Rooms

The morning after Lady Evelyn's salon, I awoke to the soft rays of sunlight filtering through the curtains, casting a warm, golden hue across my bedchamber. For a moment, I allowed myself to bask in the stillness, the remnants of sleep still clinging to my thoughts like a comforting fog. The events of the previous evening felt distant, almost dreamlike—a blur of laughter, witty repartee, and that one bold declaration that had left the room gasping before it erupted in mirth.

I smiled to myself, still rather pleased with how I had handled Lady Evelyn's challenge. Surely, by now, the gossipmongers had moved on to something else—perhaps to the latest misstep by poor Lord Fotheringay or the peculiar shade of green Lady Penelope had worn. After all, a fabricated pregnancy was amusing in the moment, but hardly something that would linger in the minds of London's elite, who had seen and heard it all.

Or so I thought.

As I dressed and prepared for the day, I felt a curious energy in the air, an almost electric undercurrent that I couldn't quite place. My maid, Alice, was uncharacteristically silent as she helped me into my morning gown, her usual cheerful chatter absent. I glanced at her, noting the way her hands trembled slightly as she fastened the buttons at my back.

"Alice, is something the matter?" I asked, frowning slightly at her unusual demeanor.

She hesitated, her gaze flicking briefly to mine before quickly looking away. "No, milady. It's just... well, there's talk in the house this morning. The servants, they've been... hearing things."

"Hearing things?" I repeated, a prickle of unease creeping up my spine. "What sort of things?"

Alice bit her lip, clearly torn between her loyalty to me and her fear of overstepping her bounds. "It's about... last night, milady. The gathering at Lady Evelyn's. There are whispers... about what you said."

I felt my heart give an involuntary lurch, though I quickly masked it with a light laugh. "Oh, that? Alice, it was just a bit of fun—a joke, nothing more."

She nodded, though her expression remained troubled. "Yes, milady. But... it seems not everyone understood it was a joke."

Her words lingered in the air like a heavy mist, refusing to dissipate. I forced myself to maintain my composure, even as a small seed of doubt began to take root in the back of my mind. Surely, people couldn't be taking the jest seriously? It had been so obvious, so outlandish, that no one with a grain of sense would believe it.

But Alice's demeanor suggested otherwise, and I couldn't shake the feeling that something was amiss.

Determined not to let this shadow my day, I dismissed Alice with a wave of my hand, reassuring her that there was nothing to worry about. "Thank you, Alice. I'll take breakfast in the drawing room this morning."

As she curtsied and left the room, I tried to focus on the day ahead, but my thoughts kept drifting back to her words. Whispers, she had said. About what I had said last night. Could it be that the guests at Lady Evelyn's salon had misunderstood my jest? Or, worse, could they have deliberately chosen to misinterpret it, twisting my words into something far more scandalous?

As I made my way to the drawing room, my steps felt heavier, weighed down by a growing sense of unease. When I entered the room, I found my brother, Edmund, already seated with a newspaper in hand, a frown etched deeply into his usually composed features.

"Good morning, Edmund," I greeted him, attempting to sound as cheerful as I could manage.

He looked up, his frown deepening as his gaze met mine. "Isabella," he said in a tone that made my heart sink. "We need to talk."

My stomach twisted with a sudden, inexplicable dread. I forced a smile, though it felt brittle at the edges. "Whatever is the matter? You look as though you've just bitten into a lemon."

Edmund set the newspaper aside, his gaze steady and unyielding. "Isabella, what exactly happened at Lady Evelyn's salon last night?"

I felt my heart skip a beat, though I managed to maintain my outward composure. "Why, nothing of consequence. We played a parlor game, and I... well, I may have made a rather cheeky announcement, but it was all in good fun."

Edmund's expression remained stony. "Cheeky? Isabella, the entire town is buzzing with the news that you announced you were... expecting."

I stared at him, my mind reeling. How had it spread so quickly? And more importantly, how had a simple joke become the talk of the town overnight?

"It was a joke, Edmund," I said, trying to keep the rising panic out of my voice. "Everyone in that room knew it was a joke."

"Apparently, not everyone," he said, his voice laced with exasperation. "I've already received three letters this morning from concerned family friends, asking for clarification. And if that weren't enough, there are whispers in every drawing room in London. People are talking, Isabella, and they're taking your words seriously."

I felt as though the ground had shifted beneath me. How could something so harmless, so clearly ridiculous, have spiraled out of control so quickly?

"But... but how?" I stammered, struggling to make sense of it all. "Surely people can't be so foolish as to believe it?"

Edmund sighed, rubbing a hand over his face. "You underestimate the power of gossip, Isabella. Once a rumor takes hold, it spreads like wildfire, and it doesn't matter how outlandish it may seem. People are more than willing to believe the worst, especially when it concerns someone of your stature."

I sank into the nearest chair, my mind spinning. I had thought myself clever, turning the dare into a performance that would be laughed off by morning. But instead, I had inadvertently set in motion a chain of events that was rapidly spiraling out of my control.

Edmund leaned forward, his tone softening slightly. "Isabella, you need to be careful. If this rumor continues to spread, it could have serious consequences—for you, for our family."

I looked up at him, a sick feeling settling in the pit of my stomach. "But what can I do? I can't exactly go door to door explaining that it was all a joke."

"No, but you can lay low for a while," Edmund suggested, his gaze steady. "Let the gossip die down on its own. Eventually, something else will come along to distract them, and this will be forgotten."

I nodded, though I wasn't entirely convinced. The problem with rumors was that they had a life of their own, growing and mutating with each retelling. And even if the scandal died down, the damage could linger.

As I sat there, grappling with the reality of what I had unwittingly unleashed, a thought struck me—one that filled me with equal parts dread and determination. If people were already talking, then it was only a matter of time before Cassian heard the rumors as well. And when he did...

I shuddered to think of the consequences.

"Edmund," I said quietly, "I think I've made a terrible mistake."

He sighed, reaching across the table to squeeze my hand. "It's not too late to fix it, Isabella. But you need to be careful from now on."

I nodded, my heart heavy with the weight of his words. I had always prided myself on my ability to navigate society's treacherous waters with grace and wit, but now I found myself caught in a current I hadn't anticipated, one that threatened to pull me under.

As the day wore on, I could feel the whispers following me, trailing behind me like a shadow I couldn't shake. Everywhere I went, I caught the glances, the raised eyebrows, the hushed conversations that ceased the moment I entered the room. It was as if I had become the center of a storm, with no way to escape its swirling vortex.

By afternoon, I had received no fewer than five visits from concerned acquaintances, each one politely inquiring after my health and hinting at the "news" they had heard. I managed to deflect their questions with vague answers and practiced smiles, but each visit left me more rattled than the last.

The whispers had taken on a life of their own, growing louder with each retelling. What had started as a joke was quickly becoming something far more insidious, and I couldn't help but wonder how long it would be before the truth was completely overshadowed by the lie.

And Cassian…

As I lay in bed that night, staring up at the darkened ceiling, I couldn't stop thinking about him. What would he say when he heard the rumors? Would he laugh it off as a harmless jest, or would he confront me, demanding answers I wasn't sure I could give?

I squeezed my eyes shut, willing the thoughts to go away, but they refused to leave me. I had made a mistake—a terrible, foolish mistake—and now I would have to face the consequences.

Little did I know, the real consequences were only just beginning to unfold.

6

A Gossip's Delight

I had always known that Lady Evelyn, the Duchess of Abernathy, was a woman who thrived on the currents of gossip that flowed through London's high society. It was her lifeblood, her entertainment, and her power. But even I, in all my caution, had underestimated just how much influence she wielded—or how easily she could turn a simple jest into something far more dangerous.

It was the morning after the salon, and I had taken Edmund's advice to heart, deciding to remain at home for the day, away from prying eyes and inquisitive tongues. I hoped that, with a bit of time and distance, the absurd rumor of my supposed pregnancy would begin to fade away, outshined by the next scandal or intrigue to capture society's fleeting attention.

But, as fate would have it, I had sorely misjudged the situation.

As I sat in the drawing room, attempting to lose myself in a book, the quiet of the morning was shattered by the sudden arrival of Lady Beatrice. She burst into the room with all the subtlety of a thunderstorm, her expression a mix of excitement and trepidation.

"Isabella," she exclaimed, not bothering with the usual pleasantries, "you won't believe what I've just heard!"

My heart sank as I set the book aside, already sensing that whatever she had to say would only add to the growing storm. "What is it, Beatrice?"

She hurried over, plopping herself down beside me on the settee. "It's Lady

Evelyn! I was at the milliner's this morning, and I happened to overhear a conversation between her and Lady Marwood."

I frowned, my stomach tightening with unease. "Lady Evelyn and Lady Marwood? That doesn't bode well. What were they talking about?"

"Nothing less than your 'delicate condition,'" Beatrice said, her voice laced with irony. "It seems that Lady Evelyn has been doing some damage control of her own, trying to downplay the rumor as a mere joke."

Relief washed over me, but it was short-lived as Beatrice continued, her tone growing more serious.

"But in the process, she may have inadvertently made things worse."

I blinked at her, trying to make sense of it all. "Worse? How could she have made it worse?"

Beatrice leaned in, her voice dropping to a conspiratorial whisper, though there was no one around to hear. "She mentioned it casually, you see—tried to laugh it off, saying that it was all part of the game, that everyone at the salon knew it was a jest. But Lady Marwood, you know how she is, always eager for a bit of scandal. She latched onto it like a dog with a bone."

My stomach churned as I imagined the scene—Lady Evelyn, likely thinking she was doing me a favor by downplaying the rumor, had instead set the stage for its spread. Lady Marwood, who had a reputation for spreading tales far and wide, would not have missed the opportunity to twist Lady Evelyn's words into something far more tantalizing.

"Oh no," I murmured, pressing a hand to my forehead. "What did Lady Marwood say?"

"She didn't need to say much," Beatrice replied, shaking her head. "She simply let Lady Evelyn's words take root in her mind, and you could practically see the wheels turning. The moment Lady Evelyn left the shop, Lady Marwood was already spinning her version of events to the other women there. And you can imagine how quickly the story will spread from there."

I closed my eyes, feeling the weight of the situation pressing down on me like a leaden cloak. What had started as a harmless joke was quickly spiraling into something much darker, much more difficult to contain. And all because Lady Evelyn, with her well-meaning attempt to dismiss the rumor, had given it new life.

Or does he have other intentions? Like deliberately dismissing the rumor by saying it's just a game, but actually making sure the rumor never dies and spreading it to the right people to keep talking about it? Thinking about it makes me break out in a cold sweat.

"But surely, people will realize it's just idle gossip," I said, though the words felt hollow even as I spoke them. "It's too ridiculous to be taken seriously."

Beatrice sighed, her expression sympathetic. "Isabella, you know as well as I do that in this world, the more ridiculous a story is, the more people want to believe it. Especially if it involves someone like you—someone who's always been so careful, so proper. It's almost as if they want to see you stumble, just to prove that you're as human as the rest of us."

I swallowed hard, the truth of her words hitting me square in the chest. I had always prided myself on my ability to navigate society's expectations with ease, to maintain my reputation without ever giving anyone reason to question it. But now, that very reputation was becoming a target, something to be poked and prodded until it cracked under the weight of scrutiny.

"What am I going to do, Beatrice?" I asked, my voice tinged with desperation. "If this continues, I'll be ruined before I even have a chance to defend myself."

Beatrice reached out and took my hand, giving it a reassuring squeeze. "We'll figure it out, Isabella. But for now, I think it's important to stay calm. The more you react, the more fuel you'll add to the fire. Maybe if we let it be, it will die down on its own."

I nodded, though my mind was racing with thoughts of what might come next. How many drawing rooms had already heard the tale? How many more would it reach before the day was out? And with each retelling, how much would the story change, twisted and exaggerated until it was unrecognizable from the truth?

As the day wore on, the full extent of the damage became clearer. By the time the afternoon sun began to dip toward the horizon, Mrs. Prendergast visited me. Her questions were veiled in politeness, but the curiosity in her eyes was unmistakable.

"It must be such a delicate time for you," Mrs. Prendergast had murmured over tea, her expression one of sympathetic concern that barely masked the eagerness in her voice. "Do take care, Lady Isabella. One's health is paramount in these situations."

I had nearly choked on my tea, managing to force a smile as I assured her that I was in perfect health and that there was nothing to worry about. But even as I spoke the words, I could see the doubt in her eyes, the way she clung to her belief in the scandal rather than accepting the truth.

The worst of it came just before dinner, when Edmund returned home after a day spent handling business in the city. He entered the drawing room with an expression that immediately set my nerves on edge—serious, composed, but with a tightness around his mouth that suggested he was holding something back.

"Isabella," he said, his tone grave, "we need to talk."

I felt a shiver of dread crawl down my spine. "What is it now?"

He sighed, running a hand through his hair before taking a seat across from me. "It seems the rumors are spreading faster than we anticipated. I spoke with several colleagues today, and it seems the story has already reached the ears of those beyond our immediate social circle. People are beginning to talk, Isabella—really talk."

My stomach twisted with anxiety. "But what are they saying? Surely they don't actually believe it?"

"It's worse than that," Edmund said, his voice laced with frustration. "They're not just believing it—they're embellishing it. Lady Evelyn's attempt to downplay the rumor has backfired spectacularly. Now, people are saying that she was trying to cover for you, that she was trying to protect your reputation."

I felt the blood drain from my face. "Protect my reputation? But that implies..."

"That implies there's something to protect," Edmund finished grimly. "People are taking her words as confirmation that the rumor is true. And Lady Marwood, bless her soul, has taken it upon herself to spread that interpretation as far and wide as she can."

I pressed a hand to my forehead, trying to process the enormity of what he was saying. "So, what do we do now? How do we stop this?"

Edmund shook his head, his expression resigned. "I'm not sure we can. Once a story like this takes hold, it's nearly impossible to squash. The best we can hope for is that it burns itself out, but that could take weeks, even months."

I stared at him, my mind reeling with the implications. I had always known that society was fickle, that gossip was a currency more valuable than gold. But I had never imagined that I would find myself at the center of such a maelstrom, with my reputation hanging by a thread.

And the worst part was, I had no one to blame but myself.

As the evening wore on, Edmund and I discussed potential strategies, though none of them seemed particularly promising. In the end, we agreed that the best course of action was to maintain a low profile, to avoid giving the gossips any more ammunition than they already had. But even as we made our plans, I couldn't shake the feeling that the damage had already been done.

By the time I retired to my chambers that night, the full weight of the situation had settled over me like a shroud. I had always prided myself on my ability to outmaneuver society's pitfalls, to maintain my composure in the face of adversity. But now, for the first time, I found myself truly afraid—afraid of what the future held, of what people would say, of what I might lose.

I couldn't help but think of Lady Evelyn, the woman who had unwittingly set this whole disaster in motion. What was she doing now? Was she laughing, amused by the chaos she had inadvertently caused? Or was she concerned, realizing that her attempt to downplay the rumor had only made it worse?

I had no answers, only a growing sense of dread that this was far from over. The story had taken on a life of its own, and I could only watch helplessly as it grew, fed by the whispers of those eager for scandal.

Little did I know, this was only the beginning.

7

An Unfortunate Encounter

The morning had started with a quiet sense of dread that I'd grown all too accustomed to. The whispers that followed me, the wary glances that were cast in my direction, and the ever-present knot of anxiety in my stomach—these had become my daily companions. But nothing could have prepared me for the encounter that awaited me as I made my way to the drawing room that afternoon, intending to take a moment of peace with a cup of tea.

As I stepped into the room, my heart sank at the sight of Duke Bastian seated comfortably in one of the armchairs, engaged in what seemed to be a deep conversation with Edmund. The two of them, once inseparable in their youth, had maintained their bond even after Bastian's marriage to Adelaide Blair. Bastian's presence had always been a comfort to me—a reminder of simpler, carefree days when the greatest worry we had was deciding which game to play in the gardens. But today, his presence was anything but comforting.

I hesitated at the doorway, my instincts screaming at me to turn and leave before he noticed me, but it was too late. Edmund looked up, catching my eye, and smiled warmly.

"Isabella," he called out, waving me over. "Come join us. Bastian was just asking after you."

Forcing a smile, I stepped further into the room, my hands clasped tightly in front of me to keep them from trembling. "Bastian," I greeted him, my voice steady despite the storm raging inside me. "It's been too long."

Bastian turned to face me, a wide grin spreading across his handsome features. He was as striking as ever, with his dark hair and sharp blue eyes, and there was a warmth in his expression that made my heart ache with nostalgia. "Isabella, it's wonderful to see you. You've been avoiding me, haven't you?" he teased lightly, rising from his chair to greet me properly.

"Of course not," I replied, managing to keep my tone light and playful. "I've just been… preoccupied."

"Preoccupied with what, exactly?" he asked, his tone turning more serious as he studied me closely. "You're not looking well, Isabella. Is everything all right?"

I forced a laugh, waving off his concern as I took a seat across from him. "I'm perfectly fine, Bastian. There's nothing to worry about."

He raised an eyebrow, clearly unconvinced. "You don't sound very convincing, you know."

Before I could respond, Edmund spoke up, a hint of amusement in his voice. "Bastian's just returned from Yorkshire, and he's already caught wind of the rumors circulating about you."

My heart skipped a beat, but I kept my expression neutral as I turned to Bastian. "Rumors?" I echoed, feigning ignorance. "What rumors?"

Bastian's gaze remained steady, his eyes searching mine for any sign of discomfort. "You know exactly what I'm talking about, Isabella," he said softly. "The rumors about you being… with child."

I could feel the color drain from my face, but I managed to keep my voice calm and steady. "Oh, that," I said, waving a dismissive hand. "It's nothing more than idle gossip, Bastian. You know how people love to talk."

He didn't respond immediately, his eyes narrowing slightly as he continued to study me. "So it's not true, then?" he asked, his tone cautious.

"Of course not," I replied firmly, refusing to let him see how rattled I truly was. "It's just a rumor, like the one that happened with Anne Blair and Colin Ashford, remember?"

At the mention of his sister-in-law, Bastian's expression softened slightly. "Yes, I remember," he said, his tone more thoughtful. "Anne shocked London with the news of her pregnancy, but it turned out to be a lie. But, she managed to get Colin Ashford in the end, right?"

I nodded, grateful for the opportunity to steer the conversation in a different direction. "Exactly. And look how that turned out—Anne and Colin are the talk of the town, and not for the reasons she originally intended. I was just copying that tactic to face a punishment at Lady Evelyn's salon. It was all in good fun."

Bastian leaned back in his chair, his expression contemplative as he considered my words. "I suppose that makes sense," he said slowly. "But you're forgetting one crucial detail, Isabella."

"What's that?" I asked, though I had a sinking feeling I already knew what he was about to say.

"In the end, Anne was pregnant," Bastian said with a soft chuckle. "Her stomach was already distended when Colin picked her up in Whitby."

I swallowed hard, forcing myself to smile as if his words hadn't sent a fresh wave of panic through me. "Yes, well, that was natural, wasn't it? Anne and Colin are husband and wife, after all. They probably did "it" while they were married. That's how Anne got pregnant."

Bastian's eyes gleamed with amusement as he leaned forward, his tone playful. "True, but it was quite the surprise, wasn't it? Even though Anne conceived after marriage, she got pregnant. That's the most important thing. And for everyone who thought it was just a ruse, finally admitting that it was true all along."

I could feel my heart pounding in my chest, but I refused to let my composure slip. "Yes, quite the surprise," I agreed, my voice calm. "But that's not the case here, Bastian. It's nothing more than a silly rumor, and it will pass, just like all the others."

Bastian studied me for a moment longer, and I could see the flicker of doubt in his eyes. But then he smiled, the tension in the room easing slightly. "If you say so, Isabella," he said, his tone light once more. "But you know you can always talk to me if something is troubling you, don't you?"

I nodded, relieved that he seemed to be accepting my explanation. "Of course, Bastian. Thank you."

Edmund, who had been silently observing our exchange, finally spoke up, his tone brisk. "Well, I think that's enough talk of rumors for one day. Let's not dwell on such nonsense."

I shot him a grateful look, eager to change the subject. "Agreed," I said, forcing a smile as I turned back to Bastian. "Tell me, how is Adelaide? And the baby?"

Bastian's expression softened at the mention of his wife and child, and I could see the pride and love in his eyes. "They're both doing wonderfully," he said, a genuine smile spreading across his face. "Adelaide is as beautiful as ever, and little Louis is growing so fast. He's already started to babble—though I'm fairly certain he's just trying to boss us all around."

I laughed, genuinely touched by the warmth in his voice. "I'm so glad to hear that. You must be very proud."

"More than I can put into words," Bastian replied, his eyes shining with affection. "They've brought so much joy into my life, Isabella. I never knew I could be this happy."

The sincerity in his words made my heart ache with a bittersweet longing. I was truly happy for Bastian, but at the same time, I couldn't help but feel a pang of envy. His life seemed so perfect, so full of love and contentment, while mine was being unraveled by a ridiculous rumor that I had unwittingly set in motion.

But I pushed those feelings aside, refusing to let them take hold. This wasn't the time to dwell on what I didn't have. I had to focus on keeping my head above water, on navigating the treacherous waters of society without sinking under the weight of the scandal that was threatening to engulf me.

As the conversation turned to lighter topics, I found myself able to relax, if only slightly. Bastian's presence, once so comforting, had become a source of tension, but I was determined not to let it show. I had managed to convince him that the rumors were nothing more than idle gossip, and for now, that was enough.

But even as I smiled and laughed along with Bastian and Edmund, a part of me couldn't shake the fear that this was only the beginning. If someone as close to me as Bastian had heard the rumors, how many others had as well?

And how long would it be before the whispers reached the ears of someone who wouldn't be so easily convinced of my innocence?

As I walked Bastian to the door later that afternoon, bidding him farewell with a smile that felt more like a mask, I couldn't help but feel a growing sense of unease. The storm was far from over, and I was only just beginning to realize how dangerous it could become.

8

The First Signs

The days following my encounter with Duke Bastian passed in a haze of strained smiles and whispered conversations. I threw myself into the mundane tasks of daily life, determined to ignore the gnawing anxiety that had taken up residence in the pit of my stomach. I attended teas, made polite conversation with acquaintances, and maintained the perfect facade of composure that society demanded.

But despite my best efforts, there was an undercurrent of tension that I couldn't quite shake. It clung to me like a shadow, lurking just out of sight, but always there, a constant reminder of the scandal that had begun to spiral out of control. The rumors had not died down as I had hoped—in fact, they seemed to be gaining momentum, whispered about in drawing rooms and discussed behind the fans of curious society ladies.

I had become the center of attention, and not in the way I had ever desired.

Still, I told myself that I could handle it. After all, I had faced the scrutiny of society before, and I had always emerged unscathed. This would be no different. I just needed to keep my wits about me, to remain calm and composed until the storm passed.

But then, something changed.

It started with a subtle fatigue, a weariness that seemed to settle into my bones. At first, I attributed it to the stress of the situation—the endless barrage of questions, the tightrope I had been walking ever since that fateful evening at Lady Evelyn's salon. But as the days went on, the fatigue deepened, becoming a constant companion that no amount of rest seemed to alleviate.

I found myself waking in the morning feeling as though I hadn't slept at all, my limbs heavy and sluggish as I struggled to go about my day. Even the simplest tasks seemed to require more effort than before, and by the time evening arrived, I was utterly drained.

But it wasn't just the fatigue. There were other signs, too—subtle, but impossible to ignore.

My appetite, once hearty and reliable, began to change. Foods that I had always enjoyed suddenly seemed unappealing, their smells and tastes turning my stomach. The rich, savory dishes that had once been my favorites now made me feel queasy, and I found myself craving simpler fare—toast, plain broth, and fresh fruit.

I tried to brush it off, telling myself that it was simply the result of nerves. After all, who wouldn't lose their appetite in the face of such a scandal? But as the days passed, I began to notice other changes, too. There was a slight nausea that lingered at the back of my throat, especially in the mornings, and an odd sense of unease that seemed to settle in my stomach, as if something wasn't quite right.

It was on a particularly gray and drizzly morning that the full weight of these changes began to press down on me.

I had woken early, as was my habit, and had gone about my morning routine as usual. But as I sat down to breakfast, the sight of the poached eggs and bacon that Alice had prepared for me sent a wave of nausea crashing over me. I had to push the plate away, my stomach churning at the mere thought of eating.

"Is everything all right, milady?" Alice asked, her voice tinged with concern as she watched me with wide eyes.

I forced a smile, though it felt more like a grimace. "I'm fine, Alice. Just not very hungry this morning."

Alice hesitated, clearly unsure whether to press the issue. "Shall I fetch you something else, milady? Perhaps some toast or fruit?"

The idea of eating anything at all made my stomach turn, but I nodded anyway, not wanting to worry her. "Yes, that would be fine, thank you."

As Alice hurried off to the kitchen, I leaned back in my chair, closing my eyes and taking a few deep breaths in an attempt to quell the nausea. But the discomfort remained, a low, persistent thrum in my abdomen that refused to be ignored.

For the first time, a sliver of doubt began to creep into my mind. I had been so certain that the changes I was experiencing were nothing more than stress, the result of the relentless pressure I had been under ever since that ill-fated evening. But now, with the nausea gnawing at me and the fatigue weighing me down, I couldn't help but wonder if there was something more to it.

But what could it be? I had always been in good health, rarely suffering from more than a mild cold or the occasional headache. There was no reason to believe that anything was seriously wrong. And yet, the symptoms persisted, growing more pronounced with each passing day.

As I sat there, staring blankly at the untouched breakfast before me, my mind began to race with possibilities. Could it be that I was coming down with an illness? But what kind of illness would cause such a strange array of symptoms—fatigue, nausea, changes in appetite? And why now, of all times?

I shook my head, dismissing the thought as quickly as it had come. It was just nerves, I told myself. Nothing more. I was under an immense amount of stress, and my body was simply reacting to that pressure. Once the scandal had died down and things had returned to normal, I would feel better.

But even as I tried to convince myself of this, a small, insistent voice at the back of my mind refused to be silenced.

What if it wasn't just nerves?

What if there was something else going on, something I hadn't yet considered?

I pushed the thought away, refusing to entertain it any further. I had enough to worry about without letting my imagination run wild. I would see how I felt over the next few days, and if the symptoms persisted, I would consult a physician. But for now, I would focus on getting through each day, one step at a time.

Alice returned a few moments later with a plate of toast and a bowl of fresh fruit, and I forced myself to take a few bites, though my stomach rebelled with every mouthful. I could see the worry in her eyes as she watched me, and I knew that she was beginning to suspect that something was wrong. But I couldn't afford to let anyone else know about the changes I was experiencing—not until I had a better understanding of what was happening.

The rest of the day passed in a blur of fatigue and unease. I went through the motions of my daily routine, attending to my duties and making polite conversation with visitors, but my mind was elsewhere, preoccupied with the strange changes in my body. The fatigue was overwhelming, a constant weight that dragged at my limbs and clouded my thoughts, and the nausea lingered at the back of my throat, a constant reminder that something wasn't right.

By the time evening arrived, I was utterly exhausted, and I retreated to my chambers earlier than usual, eager to escape the scrutiny of those around me. As I lay in bed, staring up at the darkened ceiling, my thoughts raced with a mix of fear and uncertainty. What was happening to me? Was it really just stress, or was there something more sinister at play?

And then, as I drifted off to sleep, another thought crept into my mind, one that sent a shiver of dread down my spine.

Could it be possible that…?

No. I refused to let myself finish the thought, pushing it away with a force that left me breathless. It was impossible. There was no way that could be the reason for my symptoms. It was just nerves, nothing more. I would feel better in a few days, once the scandal had blown over.

But even as I lay there, staring into the darkness, the memory of that one day with Cassian flared in my mind. A day that had been filled with passion and whispered promises—promises that I had told myself meant nothing more than a fleeting moment of weakness. We had both agreed that it was a mistake, something that could never be repeated, no matter how much we might have wanted otherwise. And yet…

What if…?

I squeezed my eyes shut, trying to banish the thought from my mind, but it was like trying to stop the tide. The memory of his touch, his voice, the way he had made me feel—it was all too real, too present. I had buried it deep, pretending that it had never happened, that it had no bearing on my life now. But now, with these changes in my body, the truth seemed to be clawing its way to the surface, refusing to be ignored any longer.

Could it really be that…?

No. I couldn't allow myself to think that way. It was just stress, nothing more. It had to be. But as I drifted off to sleep, the small, insistent voice in the back of my mind refused to be silenced.

And deep down, I knew that the truth was far more complicated than I was willing to admit.

9

A Society in Suspense

The days that followed were a strange and unsettling blur. What had once been a busy social calendar filled with invitations to teas, dinners, and soirées began to thin out, as though a subtle but undeniable shift had occurred within my circle. At first, I told myself it was simply a coincidence—after all, everyone had their own lives to lead, and perhaps the summer air had brought on a wave of unexpected obligations or illnesses. But as the invitations continued to dwindle, the reality of my situation became impossible to ignore.

The rumors had taken root, spreading through the delicate web of London society like a slow-acting poison. They began as whispers in drawing rooms and private parlors, exchanged behind the fluttering shields of lace fans, but soon they grew louder, bolder. Even when I attended the few remaining events that I was still invited to, I could feel the weight of those whispers pressing down on me, as if the very air in the room had thickened with the tension of unspoken accusations.

It was the way they looked at me that hurt the most—those speculative glances, the quick, assessing looks that darted away the moment I met their eyes. The once friendly faces of my peers had become masks of polite indifference, or worse, thinly veiled judgment. The change was subtle, like a chill in the air that you can't quite place, but it was there nonetheless, gnawing at the edges of my composure.

I would enter a room, and conversations would falter, replaced by an awkward silence that seemed to echo in my ears. When I spoke, responses were slower, more measured, as though everyone was treading carefully around me, afraid of saying the wrong thing. And when I laughed—when I tried to carry on as though nothing was amiss—it felt hollow, forced, as though I was performing a role I no longer believed in.

Even Lady Evelyn, who had been at the heart of the rumor's inception, seemed to keep her distance. I could see the flicker of something in her eyes—perhaps regret, perhaps a hint of satisfaction that her game had yielded such rich results—but she never addressed the situation directly. Instead, she remained cool and detached, watching the unfolding drama with the same calm detachment one might observe a play from the comfort of a box seat.

It was during one of these increasingly rare outings that I first noticed the full extent of the shift. Lady Beatrice had invited me to tea, a small and intimate affair with only a handful of guests, most of whom I had known for years. Normally, I would have been at ease in such a setting, surrounded by familiar faces and the warmth of good company. But on this particular afternoon, I felt anything but comfortable.

From the moment I arrived, I could sense the tension in the room. The conversations were stilted, the smiles strained. Lady Julia, who had always been one of the more talkative members of our group, seemed unusually quiet, her eyes darting between me and the others as though she were waiting for something to happen. And Lady Caroline, who was never without a kind word or a compliment, seemed preoccupied, her responses curt and perfunctory.

It was as though I had become an outsider, a curiosity to be observed but not engaged with. The familiar rhythms of our interactions had been disrupted, replaced by a sense of unease that I couldn't shake. I tried to join in the conversation, to bring some levity to the gathering with a witty remark or a humorous observation, but each attempt fell flat, met with lukewarm smiles and half-hearted chuckles.

As the tea progressed, I found myself growing increasingly anxious, the fatigue and nausea that had been plaguing me for days now compounded by the cold reception I was receiving. I could feel the eyes of the other ladies on me, watching, judging, their thoughts hidden behind those carefully composed expressions. It was as though they were all waiting for me to confirm or deny the rumors that had been swirling around me, and my refusal to acknowledge them only seemed to heighten the tension.

When the tea finally came to an end, I was both relieved and exhausted. I made my excuses, thanking Lady Beatrice for her hospitality and slipping away as quickly as I could without appearing rude. But even as I left, I could feel their eyes on my back, could hear the murmurs of conversation that resumed the moment I was out of earshot.

It was only when I returned home, the heavy door of our townhouse closing behind me, that I allowed myself to breathe freely again. I leaned against the cool wood, my heart pounding in my chest, the nausea threatening to rise once more. How had it come to this? How had a simple game—a joke, even—spiraled so far out of control?

I had thought I could handle it, that I could navigate the treacherous waters of society with the same ease and grace I always had. But now, I wasn't so sure. The isolation, the whispers, the speculative glances—it was all beginning to weigh on me, chipping away at the confidence I had always prided myself on.

And it wasn't just the social pressure. The changes in my body, the fatigue and nausea that seemed to grow worse with each passing day—they were all conspiring against me, undermining the very foundation of my carefully constructed life.

I tried to push those thoughts aside, to focus on something, anything, that would bring me back to a sense of normalcy. But the doubts remained, lurking in the corners of my mind, refusing to be silenced.

Later that evening, as I sat in my chamber, Lady Beatrice arrived unexpectedly, her expression one of deep concern. I could tell from the way she looked at me that she had noticed the changes in my behavior, the way I had been retreating more and more into myself, the weariness that had become impossible to hide.

"Isabella," she began, her voice soft and gentle, "I wanted to speak with you privately. I'm worried about you."

I forced a smile, though it felt brittle, like a thin layer of ice over a deep well of uncertainty. "There's nothing to worry about, Beatrice. I'm perfectly fine."

But she wasn't convinced. I could see it in her eyes, the way they searched mine for some sign of truth. "You're not fine," she insisted, taking a seat beside me and reaching out to take my hand. "I've known you for years, and I can tell when something is wrong. You haven't been yourself lately, and I can't help but think that this whole... situation is affecting you more than you're letting on."

I looked away, my gaze fixed on the flickering flames in the hearth, my hand tightening around hers. "It's just... everything feels so overwhelming right now," I admitted, my voice barely above a whisper. "The rumors, the way people are treating me—it's all so... suffocating."

Beatrice squeezed my hand, her expression filled with empathy. "I can only imagine how difficult this must be for you. But, you need to take care of yourself. This stress, the way you've been feeling... it's not good for you."

I swallowed hard, trying to push down the lump that had formed in my throat. "I know," I said, though the words felt hollow. "I just... I don't know how to make it stop. It's like I'm caught in this whirlwind, and no matter what I do, I can't find my way out."

Beatrice's eyes softened, and she leaned in closer, her voice low and soothing. "You don't have to go through this alone, Isabella. I'm here for you, and so is Edmund. We'll get through this together."

I nodded, though I wasn't sure I believed her. The isolation, the judgment—it all felt so overwhelming, and no matter how much I tried to reassure myself that it would pass, the doubts remained. And with them, the fear that this was only the beginning of something far more serious.

But I couldn't let Beatrice see how deeply those doubts were affecting me. She had always been my rock, the one who could see through my bravado to the vulnerable core beneath. If she knew how scared I truly was, it would only make things worse.

So, I forced another smile, this one a little steadier, and squeezed her hand in return. "Thank you, Beatrice. I appreciate your concern, truly. But I'll be all right. I just need a little time to... adjust."

She studied me for a long moment, as if weighing my words, then finally nodded, though I could tell she wasn't entirely convinced. "All right," she said softly. "But if you need anything—anything at all—you know where to find me."

"I do," I replied, my smile more genuine this time. "And I promise, I'll be fine."

But as Beatrice left, closing the door softly behind her, I felt the weight of my assurances settle heavily on my shoulders. I had told her I would be fine, but deep down, I wasn't so sure.

The whispers, the rumors, the way society was treating me—it was all beginning to take its toll. And with the strange changes in my body, the fatigue, the nausea, I couldn't help but wonder if there was something more to it all.

Something that I wasn't ready to face.

And as I sat there, staring into the flickering flames, I felt a cold knot of fear settle in my chest.

Because no matter how much I tried to convince myself otherwise, I knew that this wasn't just about the rumors. It was about something far deeper, something that had begun to unravel the life I had so carefully constructed.

And I didn't know how to stop it.

10

The Symptoms Escalate

The days following my conversation with Lady Beatrice were a torturous exercise in maintaining appearances. Each morning brought new challenges as I struggled to keep the façade of normalcy intact while my body betrayed me in ways that were becoming impossible to ignore. The subtle signs I had once dismissed as stress or nerves had grown into something undeniable, and the truth loomed closer with every passing day.

It began each morning with the familiar wave of nausea, crashing over me as soon as I opened my eyes. What had once been a mild discomfort had now intensified into something much more violent and unrelenting. The first time it happened, I barely made it to the basin in time, my body convulsing as I emptied my stomach. The retching left me weak and trembling, and the reality of my situation began to press down on me with unbearable weight.

Alice, ever the attentive maid, was the first to notice. She entered my chamber that morning to find me hunched over the basin, my hands clutching the porcelain as though it were the only thing anchoring me to reality. Her gasp of concern cut through the fog of nausea, and I looked up to see the worry etched deep into her face.

"Milady, you're not well," she said, her voice trembling as she rushed to my side. "You must rest—I'll fetch the physician at once."

"No!" The word burst from my lips with more force than I intended, laced with a panic that surprised even me. The last thing I needed was for a physician to confirm what I was already beginning to fear. "It's just a passing sickness, Alice. Nothing more. I'll be fine."

Alice hesitated, her brow furrowed in doubt as she studied me. "Are you certain, milady? You've not been yourself these past few days."

"I'm certain," I insisted, though I could feel the tremor in my voice. "It will pass. Please, just bring me some water, and I'll be right as rain."

Reluctantly, Alice complied, but the concern in her eyes remained. She returned with a glass of water, and I forced myself to drink, the cool liquid soothing my raw throat even as my stomach churned in protest. I smiled weakly at her, hoping to reassure her, but the truth was, I was far from fine.

As the days wore on, the symptoms only grew worse. The nausea that had once been confined to the mornings now lingered throughout the day, a constant reminder that something was terribly wrong. My appetite, once robust, had become erratic. Foods I had previously enjoyed turned my stomach, and I found myself craving the simplest of things—plain bread, apples, and, inexplicably, pickles, which I had never favored before. These cravings, so odd and specific, left me feeling more unsettled than ever.

It was a cruel twist of fate that the very symptoms I had once joked about had now become my reality. The whispers that had begun as a jest now felt like an ominous prophecy, one I could no longer dismiss. With each passing day, I felt the walls closing in, the weight of the secret I carried becoming too much to bear.

But despite the mounting evidence, I clung to the hope that it was all just a coincidence, that the symptoms would pass as quickly as they had come. I couldn't afford to believe otherwise—not when the truth would unravel everything I had worked so hard to maintain.

Yet, as I moved through my days, I began to notice something strange— something that added to the growing dread gnawing at my insides.

One afternoon, after a particularly grueling tea with Lady Beatrice, where I could barely keep the food down, I found myself standing alone in my chambers. The nausea had not subsided, and I felt utterly drained, both physically and mentally. I leaned against the vanity, my reflection pale and

THE SYMPTOMS ESCALATE

drawn, the dark circles under my eyes a testament to the sleepless nights and relentless anxiety.

As if on instinct, I let my hand drift to my stomach, rubbing it absently as I stared into the mirror. The gesture was one of unconscious comfort, but as my hand moved over the soft curve of my belly, a shiver of something—fear, recognition—ran through me. The sensation was foreign, unsettling. It was as if my body was trying to tell me something I wasn't ready to hear.

I froze, my hand still resting on my stomach, a cold dread creeping through my veins. Could it be...?

No. It was impossible. It had to be. But the warmth beneath my palm, the subtle firmness that hadn't been there before, whispered otherwise. I jerked my hand away as if I'd been burned, my breath catching in my throat. The gesture, so simple, had confirmed what I had been desperately trying to deny.

I was changing. My body was changing. And with it, the life I had known was slipping away.

The symptoms were worsening, and with them, my ability to maintain the charade. The fatigue, the cravings, the morning sickness—all of it was pointing to the same inevitable conclusion. The fear that I had so carefully suppressed was now bubbling to the surface, threatening to overwhelm me.

I couldn't keep this up much longer. The symptoms, the whispers, the growing suspicion in the eyes of those around me—it was all becoming too much to bear. And the worst part was, I still didn't know for certain what was happening to me, though the truth was becoming harder and harder to deny.

As the afternoon wore on, I found myself growing more and more fatigued, the nausea a constant companion that refused to leave my side. By the time I returned home, I was utterly spent, and I retreated to my chambers with a sense of dread that I couldn't shake.

I sat down on the edge of my bed, my hand again drifting to my stomach where it lingered, the touch both comforting and terrifying. There was no denying the subtle changes I felt beneath my fingertips, the slight swelling that had not been there before becoming more apparent. And with that realization came the crushing weight of what it meant.

As I lay in bed that night, staring up at the darkened ceiling, the thoughts

I had been trying to avoid for so long finally broke through the dam I had built around them. The nausea, the fatigue, the cravings—they were all too familiar, too reminiscent of the very thing I had been joking about not so long ago.

And as the truth settled over me like a suffocating blanket, I felt the tears slip down my cheeks, silent and unchecked.

Maybe I was pregnant.

The realization hit me like a tidal wave, crashing over me with a force that left me gasping for breath. I had known, deep down, that this was the only explanation that made sense, but I had been too afraid to admit it, even to myself.

But now, there was no denying it. The symptoms were too pronounced, too specific, to be anything else. And as I lay there, the full weight of what this meant began to sink in.

I was pregnant, and the father was Cassian.

The man I had tried so hard to forget, the man whose touch still lingered in my memory, the man whose name was now inextricably linked to the scandal that had begun as a joke but had turned into a nightmare.

I didn't know what to do. I didn't know how to face the truth, how to navigate the treacherous waters of society with this new burden weighing me down. All I knew was that everything had changed, and there was no going back.

And as the night stretched on, the tears continued to fall, each one a silent testament to the fear and uncertainty that now consumed me. My hand remained on my stomach, as if trying to comprehend the life that was growing inside me—the life that would change everything.

The truth was out now, even if only within the confines of my own heart. And with it came the terrifying realization that I could no longer hide from what was to come.

11

A Passionate Picnic

My mind couldn't help but wander back to the beginning—the night it all started. My thoughts drifted back to that evening, months ago, when everything was so different, so uncomplicated. Back then, the idea of anything more than a flirtation with Cassian seemed impossible, even absurd. But I'd been wrong, and now I was facing the consequences of a choice that had seemed so small at the time.

It was at a lavish soirée hosted by the Marquess of Waverly, a gathering that had promised nothing more than the usual rounds of polite conversation, shared gossip, and champagne. I hadn't expected to see Cassian there, not after his recent return to London following an extended stay in the countryside. He had always been a charming rogue, a man with an easy smile and a wit that could cut through the thickest of social pretenses. But that night, there was something different about him—an intensity in his gaze that I couldn't quite place.

We hadn't spoken in months, not since our last encounter at a ball where we'd exchanged little more than pleasantries. But that evening, as I wandered away from the crowded ballroom in search of a quiet moment, I found myself face-to-face with Cassian in the Marquess's study. The room was dimly lit, the scent of tobacco and old leather hanging in the air, and he was leaning casually against the mantelpiece, a glass of brandy in his hand.

"Lady Isabella," he greeted me, his voice low and warm. "Escaping the chaos, I see."

I smiled, suddenly self-conscious under the weight of his gaze. "Just for a moment. It can be rather overwhelming, can't it?"

He nodded, taking a slow sip of his drink. "Indeed. Sometimes it's nice to step away, to have a moment of clarity."

His words felt laden with meaning, though I wasn't sure what that meaning was. We chatted for a while, the conversation light but with an undercurrent of something more. It was different from our usual banter—there was a tension, a spark that hadn't been there before. I found myself drawn to him, more so than I had ever been, and I couldn't help but wonder if he felt the same.

Before the evening was over, Cassian suggested we meet again, away from the prying eyes of society. It was a bold request, one that I might have refused under different circumstances. But that night, something inside me craved the thrill of it, the idea of stepping outside the bounds of propriety, if only for a little while.

We met a few days later at a secluded café in Mayfair, a place known for its discretion. The kind of place where the well-to-do conducted their secret affairs, away from the prying eyes of London's elite. Cassian was waiting for me when I arrived, a smile playing on his lips as he stood to greet me.

"I wasn't sure you'd come," he admitted as we sat down, the flickering candlelight casting shadows across his features.

"Neither was I," I replied honestly, my heart racing in my chest. "But I'm here."

Our conversation flowed easily, the barriers between us slipping away as the evening wore on. We spoke of everything and nothing—his time in the countryside, my family's recent ventures, the latest gossip from the ton. But beneath it all, there was an unspoken connection, a shared understanding that this was more than just a casual meeting.

After that night, we met several more times, each encounter more clandestine than the last. There was something intoxicating about the secrecy, about the way we had to carefully plan our meetings to avoid suspicion. It was as if we were playing a dangerous game, one that only we understood the rules to.

And with each meeting, I found myself falling deeper into whatever it was that existed between us.

Our rendezvous took us to quiet corners of the city, to parks and gardens where we could walk and talk without fear of being overheard. We met in a small bookshop once, tucked away in an alley where no one would think to look for us. It was there that Cassian first kissed me, a brief but intense moment that left me breathless, my heart pounding in my chest as I realized just how far this had gone.

But it was on a warm afternoon at a secluded estate outside of London that everything changed. We had met there under the guise of a picnic, a chance to enjoy the countryside away from the pressures of the city. The estate belonged to a distant cousin of Cassian's, a place where he knew we would be undisturbed.

The day was perfect—sunlight streaming through the trees, a gentle breeze rustling the leaves. We spread out a blanket on the grass, the sounds of nature providing the perfect backdrop to our conversation. But as the afternoon wore on, the playful banter gave way to something deeper, something neither of us could ignore any longer.

"I can't stop thinking about you," Cassian confessed, his voice low as he leaned closer to me. "Every time we part, all I can think about is when I'll see you again."

His words sent a shiver down my spine, my own feelings mirrored in his confession. "I feel the same," I admitted, my voice barely above a whisper. "But this... whatever this is... it's dangerous, Cassian."

"Dangerous, perhaps," he agreed, his hand brushing against mine. "But isn't it also thrilling?"

I didn't have a chance to answer before his lips were on mine, the kiss deep and urgent, fueled by the weeks of tension that had been building between us. My heart raced as I returned the kiss, my hands tangling in his hair as I lost myself in the moment.

One kiss led to another, and before I knew it, we were no longer just two people enjoying a picnic. We were lovers, caught up in a passion that had been simmering beneath the surface for far too long. The secluded grove provided the privacy we needed, the soft grass beneath us cushioning our descent as we gave in to the desires we had both been fighting.

He removed my layered dress, revealing my corset and petticoats underneath. His fingers traced the curves of my body, sending shivers down my spine. I undid his trousers, freeing his hard cock. We made love on the soft grass, our bodies moving in perfect harmony.

We sat down on the soft grass, and I straddled him, feeling his length press against me. I moaned as he entered me, filling me completely. We moved together, our bodies slick with sweat, our moans and sighs mingling with the sounds of nature around us.

He thrust deeper and harder, his cock slapping against my ass. I could feel myself getting closer and closer to the edge.

And then, with one final thrust, I came, my pussy clenching around his cock, milking it for all it was worth. He followed soon after, his hot cum filling me up.

After a while, Cassian switched positions by laying me on the grass and undressing me completely. He kissed every inch of my body, his tongue exploring every curve and crevice. I writhed beneath him, my fingers tangled in his hair.

Cassian hovered above me, a fierce silhouette against the dappled sunlight, his eyes reflecting the primal need that coursed through both of us. His lips found mine once more, in a kiss that sealed our silent vows, before trailing a burning path down my neck, pausing to savor the beat of my racing heart. I couldn't contain the gasps that escaped as he worshiped my body, his tongue licking my heated skin.

The world reduced to the space where our bodies met, time measured only in breaths and heartbeats. As he entered me, there was nothing gentle about it—only a fierce claiming that spoke of raw need and an intimacy that words could never capture. The rhythm he set was relentless, each thrust sending shockwaves of pleasure coursing through me. I cried out with pleasure. He thrust deep and hard, our bodies slapping together in a primal rhythm. I moaned, my nails digging into his back.

He reached down, rubbing my clit in slow circles. I could feel the pressure building inside me, my orgasm just out of reach.

"My lady," he whispered, his breath hot against my ear.

And with that, I let go, my body shuddering with pleasure as I came hard around his cock. He followed soon after, his hot seed filling me up.

We lay there, spent and satisfied, our bodies entwined, our hearts beating as one. It was a moment I would never forget, a moment that would forever be etched in my memory.

We stood in that secluded grove, the sun setting behind the trees, casting long shadows across the grass. He reached out to me, his hand trembling slightly as he brushed a stray curl from my face. "Isabella!" He whispered, my voice thick with emotion, "I—"

It was a moment of pure abandon, one that I couldn't bring myself to regret, even now. But as the sun began to set, reality came crashing back. Cassian had to leave for Birmingham the next day, called away to tend to his family's business—a thriving textile enterprise that kept him busy, especially as the second son, with no title to inherit. We parted ways that evening, both of us knowing that things had changed between us, but neither of us willing to acknowledge just how much.

I hadn't seen him since that day. His letters had been sparse, and I had told myself it was better this way—that we both needed the distance to regain our senses, to remind ourselves of the boundaries we had crossed.

The man who had left me behind, who had no idea what had happened in his absence. The man whose name was now forever linked to mine in a way that neither of us could have anticipated.

Tears slipped down my cheeks as the full weight of the situation settled over me, the fear and uncertainty almost too much to bear. I didn't know what to do, how to face the future that was now so terrifyingly uncertain. All I knew was that nothing would ever be the same again.

And as the night stretched on, the tears continued to fall, each one a silent testament to the reality I could no longer avoid.

12

The Rumor's Reach

The morning dawned gray and heavy, the sky a sheet of unbroken cloud that seemed to mirror the weight pressing down on my chest. I had spent the night tossing and turning, haunted by the realization that had struck me like a thunderclap—there was no denying it now. I was pregnant, and the implications of that truth were beginning to spiral out of my control.

I had barely managed to close my eyes when the knock came at my door. It was Alice, of course, as punctual as ever, but there was a tension in her demeanor that immediately set me on edge.

"Milady," she began, her voice tinged with a mixture of urgency and concern, "your brother, Lord Edmund, requests your presence in the drawing room. He says it's of utmost importance."

A chill ran down my spine at her words. Edmund's summons were rarely delivered with such gravity, and I knew that whatever awaited me downstairs would not be a simple morning conversation.

"I'll be down shortly, Alice," I replied, keeping my voice as steady as I could manage. "Please help me dress."

As she moved to retrieve my gown for the day, I tried to focus on the mundane task ahead—dressing, preparing to face whatever it was that Edmund had to say—but the pounding of my heart drowned out my attempts at calm. My thoughts raced, leaping to the worst possible conclusions. Could it be that the rumor had spread even further than I'd feared? Had someone, in their eagerness to fan the flames of scandal, taken the story beyond the circles of London society and delivered it directly into the ears of those who could not afford to ignore it?

Alice returned with a gown of dark green silk, elegant and understated, but as she began to help me into it, I felt a strange discomfort settle in my stomach. The pressure of the fabric against my abdomen was suddenly unbearable, as if the very act of dressing was forcing me to confront the reality I had been trying so hard to ignore.

"Milady?" Alice asked, noticing my wince as she tightened the laces. "Are you all right?"

I nodded, though the movement felt forced, my breath coming in shallow gasps as the corset pressed against my stomach. The discomfort was not just physical—it was as though the constriction of the gown was a mirror to the suffocating pressure I felt within, the weight of the secret I carried threatening to crush me from the inside out.

"Yes, Alice, I'm fine," I lied, forcing a smile. "It's just... a little tight this morning. Could you loosen it, please?"

Alice hesitated, her eyes narrowing with concern, but she complied, loosening the laces just enough to relieve the pressure. The relief was immediate, but it did little to ease the growing sense of dread that curled in the pit of my stomach.

Once dressed, I stood before the mirror, taking a moment to compose myself. The woman who stared back at me was a shadow of the Isabella Fairchild I had once known—her skin pale, her eyes dull and haunted. I had always prided myself on my ability to face the world with grace and poise, but now, even the simplest task of getting dressed felt like an insurmountable burden.

"Milady," Alice said softly, breaking the silence, "Lord Edmund is waiting."

I nodded again, smoothing the fabric of my gown with trembling hands before turning to leave the room. The journey to the drawing room felt interminable, each step weighted with the fear of what awaited me. By the time I reached the door, my breath was shallow, and my heart hammered so loudly in my chest that I was certain it would give me away.

I paused for a moment, steeling myself before pushing open the door and stepping inside.

Edmund was waiting for me in the drawing room, his posture rigid as he stood by the window, staring out at the gray sky beyond. His silhouette against the dull light was imposing, a reflection of the tension that had been building since the rumors began to circulate. When he finally turned to face me, his expression was unreadable, but the tension in his jaw spoke volumes. This was not going to be a pleasant conversation.

"Isabella," he began, his voice carefully controlled, his tone formal in a way that made my heart skip a beat. "We need to talk."

I forced myself to remain calm, even as anxiety gnawed at the edges of my composure. I couldn't let him see how nervous I was. "Of course, Edmund," I replied, striving to keep my voice steady as I moved to take a seat. "What's this all about?"

He didn't join me, instead choosing to remain standing, his arms crossed over his chest as he regarded me with a stern gaze. "I've just received a letter," he said, his tone clipped, each word delivered with precision, "from the palace."

The words hung in the air between us, and I felt my stomach drop. The cold dread I had been trying to keep at bay all morning came rushing back with a vengeance. "From the palace?" I echoed, my voice barely above a whisper. "What... what did it say?"

Edmund's eyes narrowed, and he took a step closer, his expression hardening. "It seems the rumor about your... condition has reached the ears of the royal family."

My breath caught in my throat, and for a moment, I felt as though the room was spinning around me. The royal family—the very idea that they would concern themselves with such gossip was unthinkable. And yet, here it was, the proof of just how far the rumor had spread.

"They are... concerned," Edmund continued, his voice growing sharper, "concerned that a member of their extended family might be involved in a scandal of this magnitude. They've requested a meeting to... clarify the situation."

My heart pounded in my chest, the walls of the room closing in on me as the full weight of the situation pressed down. This was no longer a matter of idle gossip—this was a matter of serious consequence, one that could affect not just me, but our entire family.

"Isabella," Edmund said, his voice cutting through the haze of panic that had enveloped me, "I need to know the truth. Is there any truth to these rumors?"

His eyes bore into mine, demanding an answer that I wasn't prepared to give. I opened my mouth to speak, but the words caught in my throat, my mind racing as I searched for something—anything—that could explain away the situation without revealing the truth.

But there was nothing. No clever lie, no half-truth that could shield me from the reality of what was happening. The truth was that I might really be pregnant, and the father was Cassian, and there was no way to spin that in a way that would satisfy the royal family—or anyone else, for that matter.

"Isabella," Edmund pressed, his voice growing more urgent, "you need to tell me the truth. If there's any chance of mitigating the damage, I need to know exactly what we're dealing with."

I met his gaze, and for a moment, I thought about confessing everything. The weight of the secret I had been carrying was too much to bear, and now, with the threat of royal intervention hanging over my head, it was all I could do to keep from collapsing under the pressure. But as I looked into his eyes, the words died on my lips. I couldn't do it. I couldn't bring myself to admit the truth, to see the disappointment and anger in his eyes, to confirm the rumors that would bring shame not just to me, but to our entire family.

"I... I don't know how to explain it," I whispered, my voice trembling. "I never meant for this to happen, Edmund. It was just... a mistake."

His eyes widened in shock, and for a moment, he said nothing, the silence between us growing heavier with each passing second. When he finally spoke, his voice was tight with barely controlled anger. "You're telling me that the rumors are true?"

I couldn't answer, I just shook my head repeatedly. The tears welling up in my eyes as I looked away, unable to face the disappointment in his gaze. But I also couldn't bring myself to confirm it. The truth was too overwhelming, too final. I needed time—time to figure out what to do, time to find a way to salvage the situation without losing everything.

"No... the rumors are not true," I said trying to calm Edmund down or actually I was calming myself down.

"For God's sake, Isabella," Edmund hissed, running a hand through his hair in frustration. "Do you have any idea what this means? What you've done?"

I shook my head, my shoulders shaking with silent sobs as the enormity of the situation crashed over me. I had known, of course, that the truth would come out eventually, but I hadn't been prepared for the reality of it—the shame, the fear, the knowledge that I had not only jeopardized my own reputation but had also placed our entire family in danger.

Edmund began pacing the room, his anger palpable as he struggled to come to terms with what he believed to be the truth. "We need to think," he muttered, more to himself than to me. "We need to find a way to control this before it gets any worse."

I remained silent, my hands clenching the fabric of my gown as I tried to regain some semblance of composure. But the truth was, I had no idea how to fix this. I had been so focused on keeping the secret that I hadn't considered what would happen when it finally came to light—or when it was suspected.

"Isabella," Edmund said, finally stopping in front of me, his voice low and tense, "we're going to have to face this head-on. There's no avoiding it now. The royal family is involved, and we need to tread carefully if we want to avoid complete ruin."

I looked up at him, my heart breaking at the sight of the pain and frustration etched into his features. This wasn't just about me anymore—it was about our entire family, and the future that had once seemed so secure was now hanging by a thread.

"I'm sorry, Edmund," I whispered, my voice choked with emotion.

He sighed, his expression softening slightly as he placed a hand on my shoulder. "I know, Isabella. But we don't have the luxury of regret now. We have to act—and we have to act fast."

I nodded, though the fear still gripped me like a vice, making it difficult to think, let alone make a plan. But I knew he was right. The situation had spiraled out of my control, and if we didn't find a way to manage it, the consequences would be catastrophic.

As we stood there, the weight of the world pressing down on us both, I couldn't help but wonder how it had come to this—how a single mistake had led to a situation that threatened to destroy everything we held dear.

And as I met Edmund's gaze, I knew that whatever happened next, I couldn't bring myself to confess. The truth was too heavy, too fraught with consequences. But deep down, I knew that my silence would only delay the inevitable. The storm was coming, and we would have to face it—together.

13

The Uncomfortable Truth

The days that followed my conversation with Edmund were a blur of tension and mounting dread. The knowledge that the royal family had become aware of the rumors surrounding me was like a noose tightening around my neck. Every breath I took felt constricted, not just by the corset I wore, but by the suffocating pressure of the scandal that threatened to engulf me.

Each morning, as Alice helped me into my corset, I found myself dreading the moment when the laces would tighten, pressing against my abdomen in a way that was becoming increasingly unbearable. The size that had once fit me perfectly now felt like a prison, each pull of the laces a reminder of the changes happening within my body—changes I was desperately trying to ignore.

"A little tighter, milady?" Alice asked one morning, her fingers deftly working the laces with the practiced ease of someone who had performed this task countless times before.

"Yes, Alice, as usual," I replied, forcing a smile as I gripped the edge of the vanity to steady myself. The truth was, I could hardly bear the thought of the corset tightening further, but I didn't want to raise any suspicion. Alice had served me faithfully for years, and I knew that she could read me better than anyone. The last thing I needed was for her to start asking questions I wasn't ready to answer.

As the laces pulled taut, I felt my breath catch in my throat. The pressure was intense, pressing down on my stomach like a vice. I closed my eyes, willing myself to remain composed, to push through the discomfort as I had done every day since the symptoms had begun.

"There we are," Alice said, tying off the laces with a satisfied nod. "You look lovely as always, milady."

"Thank you, Alice," I murmured, my voice tight as I struggled to take a full breath. The room felt stifling, the air thick with the scent of lavender that suddenly seemed overwhelming.

With the corset secured, Alice helped me into my dress, a deep blue silk that normally would have brought out the color of my eyes. Today, however, I could barely focus on my reflection in the mirror. All I could think about was the constriction around my waist, the way each breath seemed to require more effort than the last.

"Are you sure you're all right, milady?" Alice asked, her brow furrowing as she caught sight of my pale face. "You don't look well."

"I'm fine, Alice," I lied, forcing another smile as I smoothed the fabric of my dress. "Just a bit tired, that's all."

She didn't look convinced, but she nodded anyway, stepping back to give me space. "If you need anything, please don't hesitate to call for me."

"I will," I assured her, though in truth, I could hardly wait for her to leave the room so I could be alone with my thoughts.

With the dress finally in place, I took a deep breath—though it was more of a shallow gasp, given the tightness of the corset—and made my way downstairs to meet Lady Beatrice. We had plans to visit one of the more fashionable shops in town, and I had no choice but to go through with it, despite the growing discomfort that gnawed at my insides.

As I stepped outside into the cool morning air, I hoped that the fresh air would help alleviate the dizziness that had begun to creep over me. But with each step, the world around me seemed to blur, the edges of my vision darkening as the pressure on my stomach grew more unbearable.

"You're very quiet today, Isabella," Beatrice observed as we walked, her voice laced with concern. "Are you certain you're all right?"

"Just a bit tired," I repeated, the words feeling hollow even as I spoke them. I could feel the sweat beginning to bead on my forehead, and I resisted the urge to wipe it away, not wanting to draw attention to my discomfort.

As we entered the shop, I was immediately struck by the warmth of the interior, the heat from the fireplace making the air feel even more stifling. My head swam, and I had to grip the edge of a nearby table to steady myself.

"Isabella, you're as pale as a ghost," Beatrice exclaimed, her eyes widening with alarm. "You really don't look well at all."

"I... I think I need to sit down," I managed to say, my voice faint as the room began to spin. The corset felt like it was squeezing the very life out of me, each breath a struggle as I fought to stay conscious.

Beatrice quickly guided me to a chair, her hand on my arm as she called for a glass of water. "You need to take care of yourself, Isabella," she said, her tone firm but kind. "This isn't like you at all."

I nodded weakly, my vision blurring as I sipped the water that was brought to me. The cool liquid did little to ease the tightness in my chest, and I knew I couldn't stay much longer.

"I'm sorry, Beatrice," I whispered, my voice trembling with the effort of speaking. "I think I need to go home."

"Of course," she said immediately, signaling for the carriage. "I'll take you home right away."

The ride back to the townhouse was a blur of discomfort and exhaustion. I could barely focus on anything but the tightness around my waist, the way each breath felt like a battle against the constriction of the corset. By the time we arrived, I was so pale and drained that I could hardly stand.

Alice was waiting for me at the door, her eyes widening in shock as she took in my appearance. "Milady, what happened? You look like you're about to faint!"

"I just need to lie down," I managed to say, my voice weak as I clung to the doorframe for support. "Please, help me out of this dress."

Without another word, Alice hurried to assist me, her fingers working quickly to undo the buttons and laces that had become my prison. As the corset finally loosened, I gasped for breath, the relief almost overwhelming as the pressure on my stomach eased.

"Milady, you're sweating," Alice said, her voice filled with concern as she helped me out of the dress and into a loose, comfortable gown. "You should rest. I'll bring you some tea."

"Thank you, Alice," I whispered, too exhausted to argue as I sank into the softness of my bed.

Alone in my chamber, I finally allowed myself to acknowledge the fear that had been gnawing at me for weeks. The symptoms—the nausea, the dizziness, the growing discomfort in my own body—were no longer something I could dismiss as mere stress.

As I lay there, my hand resting lightly on my stomach, I couldn't help but think back to that brief, passionate affair with Cassian Cavendish. The memory of his touch, his whispered promises, had been something I'd tried to push aside, telling myself it was nothing more than a fleeting indiscretion. But now, with the evidence of my condition becoming harder to ignore, I began to piece together the timeline.

Could it be that the symptoms I'd been experiencing were a result of that day? The possibility sent a chill through me, the implications too terrifying to fully grasp.

I closed my eyes, my heart pounding with a mixture of fear and uncertainty. The signs were all there, pointing to a truth I wasn't ready to accept. And yet, deep down, I knew that I couldn't keep running from it. The corset that had once been a shield against the world now felt like a cruel reminder of the life growing inside me—a life that would change everything.

As the day turned to evening, and the darkness settled over the room, I finally allowed myself to face the reality of my situation. Maybe I was really pregnant, and the father was Cassian—a man whose very name was now intertwined with the scandal that had begun as a joke but had spiraled into something far more dangerous.

The tears that had been threatening all day finally spilled over, silent and unchecked, as I lay there in the solitude of my chamber. I didn't know how I would navigate the treacherous waters ahead, but one thing was certain: my life would never be the same.

14

Confessions and Revelations

The weight of my secret had become unbearable, a heavy burden that seemed to grow with each passing day. I could no longer ignore the signs—the nausea, the dizziness, the way my body had begun to change in ways that I could no longer dismiss as mere stress. The tightness of my corset, once a symbol of control and dignity, had transformed into a cruel reminder of the life growing within me. And as the days wore on, the truth I had been so desperate to avoid became undeniable.

I knew I couldn't keep this to myself any longer. The fear and uncertainty were gnawing at me, consuming my thoughts and leaving me feeling more isolated than ever before. I needed to confide in someone—someone I trusted, who could help me make sense of the turmoil swirling inside me. And there was only one person who came to mind.

Lady Beatrice had always been my closest friend, the one person who knew me better than anyone else. We had shared countless secrets over the years, but nothing had ever come close to the gravity of what I was about to reveal. Still, I knew I had no choice. I couldn't bear the uncertainty alone any longer.

The decision to confide in Beatrice came one afternoon when the tension in my chest had become too much to bear. I had asked her to visit me at home, under the guise of a simple tea, but my heart raced with the knowledge that this conversation would be anything but ordinary.

As we sat in the drawing room, the familiar scent of roses and the gentle clinking of porcelain providing a semblance of normalcy, I struggled to find the words. Beatrice, ever perceptive, sensed my unease and set her teacup down, her brow furrowing with concern.

"Isabella, what's wrong?" she asked softly, her gaze searching mine. "You've been so distant lately, and I can't help but feel that something is troubling you."

I took a deep breath, my hands trembling as I set my own teacup down, the liquid inside rippling slightly from the unsteadiness of my grip. The room suddenly felt too warm, the walls closing in around me as I gathered the courage to speak.

"Beatrice," I began, my voice barely above a whisper, "I... I need to tell you something. Something I've been trying to deny, but... I can't do it anymore."

She leaned forward, her eyes wide with concern. "Isabella, you're scaring me. What is it?"

The words caught in my throat, but I knew I couldn't turn back now. I had to tell her everything. "I think... I think I might be pregnant," I confessed, my voice trembling with the weight of the admission.

For a moment, Beatrice simply stared at me, her expression one of shock and disbelief. "Pregnant?" she repeated, as if the word itself was foreign. "But... how...?"

Her question hung in the air, and I knew there was no avoiding the truth. My heart pounded in my chest as I forced myself to continue. "It happened a few months ago, during that brief affair with Cassian Cavendish. We... we were careless, and now I think I'm... I'm with child."

Beatrice's eyes widened even further, her hand flying to her mouth as the shock of my confession settled in. "Isabella... oh, my dear Isabella," she whispered, her voice filled with a mixture of disbelief and concern. "Why didn't you tell me sooner?"

"I didn't want to believe it," I admitted, my voice breaking as the tears I had been holding back finally spilled over. "I thought... I thought it was just stress, that it would all go away. But the signs... they've only grown stronger, and now... now I'm terrified, Beatrice."

Without a word, Beatrice moved from her seat to sit beside me, wrapping her arms around me in a comforting embrace. The warmth of her presence was a balm to my frayed nerves, and for the first time in weeks, I allowed myself to truly cry, the weight of my fear and uncertainty pouring out in a torrent of emotion.

As the sobs subsided, Beatrice pulled back slightly, her eyes filled with compassion. "We'll figure this out together, Isabella," she said firmly. "You don't have to go through this alone."

I nodded, grateful for her support, but the fear still gnawed at me. "I'm so afraid, Beatrice," I whispered, my voice trembling. "My belly... it's starting to grow. I can feel it. The corset—every day it feels tighter, more unbearable. I can't hide it much longer."

Her eyes softened with understanding, and she reached for my hand, giving it a reassuring squeeze. "Let me see," she said gently. "If we're going to face this, we need to know for sure."

The idea of revealing the changes in my body filled me with a deep sense of dread, but I knew she was right. We needed to confirm what I had been fearing for weeks. My hands shook as I reached for the laces of my corset, my breath catching in my throat as I began to unfasten them.

Beatrice watched me closely, her expression a mixture of concern and determination. As I loosened the laces, the pressure around my stomach eased, and I felt a strange mixture of relief and fear. The corset, which had once been a source of security, now felt like a prison I was finally escaping from.

When the laces were finally undone, I hesitated, my hands trembling as I slowly lifted the fabric of my chemise to reveal my stomach. The sight that met my eyes made my breath catch in my throat—a small, but unmistakable mound, hard and unyielding beneath my fingertips.

Beatrice gasped softly, her eyes widening in shock as she took in the sight. "Isabella," she whispered, her voice filled with a mixture of awe and fear. "This... this is real."

I nodded, tears welling up in my eyes as I placed a trembling hand on the small bump. The reality of my situation hit me like a tidal wave, the enormity of what was happening crashing over me with a force that left me breathless.

"What am I going to do, Beatrice?" I asked, my voice breaking with emotion. "How am I going to hide this? How am I going to face the consequences?"

Beatrice was silent for a moment, her gaze fixed on the small mound that had become the undeniable proof of my condition. Then, with a deep breath, she looked up at me, her expression resolute.

"The first thing we need to do," she said firmly, "is confirm the pregnancy. We need to know for sure, so we can make a plan. I'll help you, Isabella. We'll get through this together, but we need to be certain."

I nodded, though the thought of confirming what I already knew filled me with dread. But Beatrice was right—we needed to know for sure, and we needed to do it soon. The longer we waited, the more difficult it would be to keep the secret.

"We'll go to the physician tomorrow," Beatrice continued, her voice calm and steady. "I'll come with you. We'll find out for certain, and then we'll figure out what to do next."

I felt a surge of gratitude for her support, but the fear still lingered, gnawing at the edges of my resolve. "What if... what if he confirms it?" I whispered, my voice barely audible. "What will I do then?"

Beatrice reached out to take my hand, her grip firm and reassuring. "Then we'll face it together," she said softly. "You're not alone in this, Isabella. We'll find a way to get through it, no matter what."

Her words brought a small measure of comfort, but the fear and uncertainty still weighed heavily on my heart. The thought of what lay ahead—the implications of my condition, the scandal it would bring, the consequences that would follow—filled me with a sense of dread that I couldn't shake.

As Beatrice helped me fasten the corset again, her hands gentle and careful not to tighten it too much, I felt the tears slip down my cheeks once more. The corset, now loosened, still felt like a burden, a symbol of the life I had once known slipping away. And as we prepared to face the truth together, I knew that my life was about to change in ways I had never imagined.

But with Beatrice by my side, I felt a small flicker of hope, a glimmer of strength that I hadn't known I possessed. We would face the truth together, and no matter what happened, I knew that I wouldn't have to bear the burden alone.

    As the evening drew to a close, and I found myself once more alone in my chamber, the reality of what lay ahead began to settle over me. The small mound on my stomach was no longer something I could ignore, no longer a sign that could be dismissed as mere stress or nerves. It was real, and it was growing, and soon, the whole world would know.

15

The Unveiling Truth

The next morning dawned with a sense of foreboding that I couldn't shake. The skies were overcast, a dull gray that matched the heavy weight in my chest as Beatrice and I prepared to leave for our clandestine visit to the physician. The entire process felt surreal, as if I were moving through a dream—or perhaps a nightmare—from which I could not wake.

Beatrice arrived early, her presence a welcome balm to my frayed nerves. Her expression was calm but serious, a reflection of the gravity of the situation we were about to face together. I appreciated her strength more than I could say, knowing that without her, I might not have had the courage to follow through.

As we stepped into the carriage, I felt the tension coiling tighter in my stomach, the reality of what we were about to do sinking in deeper with each passing moment. The ride to the outskirts of the city seemed to stretch on endlessly, the silence between us heavy with unspoken fears.

When we finally arrived at the small, nondescript house that belonged to the physician, I felt a wave of apprehension wash over me. The building itself was unremarkable, tucked away from prying eyes, but to me, it might as well have been a grand courthouse where my fate would be decided.

Beatrice squeezed my hand as we approached the door, offering me a reassuring smile. "It's going to be all right, Isabella," she murmured, though the tension in her voice betrayed her own anxiety. "We're just here to confirm what we already know, and then we can make a plan."

I nodded, though my throat felt too tight to speak. My heart pounded in my chest as we stepped inside, the air cool and still, carrying with it the faint scent of herbs and medicine.

The physician, a man in his late middle age with graying hair and kind eyes, greeted us with a calm demeanor that did little to ease my nerves. His name was Dr. Turner, and he came highly recommended by Beatrice's distant cousin—a connection that ensured our visit would remain discreet.

"Lady Isabella, Lady Beatrice," Dr. Turner greeted us with a respectful nod as we entered his office. "I understand you're here for a matter of some delicacy."

"Yes, Doctor," I replied, my voice trembling slightly despite my best efforts to remain composed. "I... I need to confirm whether I am with child."

He gave a gentle, understanding nod. "Of course, my lady. Please, have a seat, and we'll conduct the examination."

The formality of the situation only heightened my anxiety, but I did as he asked, taking a seat on the examination table. The room was small and sparsely furnished, with a single window that let in a dim light. It felt as though the walls were closing in around me, the air growing thinner as I struggled to steady my breathing.

Dr. Turner moved with a quiet efficiency, asking a few preliminary questions about my symptoms and the timing of my last monthly courses. His manner was professional and respectful, but I couldn't help but feel exposed, vulnerable in a way I had never experienced before.

"Would you please remove your dress and corset, Lady Isabella?" Dr. Turner asked, his tone gentle but firm. "I'll need to examine your abdomen to assess the situation."

The request sent a fresh wave of discomfort through me, but I complied, my hands trembling as I unfastened the buttons of my dress and shrugged out of it. Beatrice stood by my side, her expression a mixture of concern and determination as she helped me with the corset. The moment it loosened, I felt a strange mix of relief and dread—relief from the suffocating pressure, and dread for what would come next.

With my chemise still covering me, I lay back on the examination table, my heart racing as Dr. Turner approached. He placed a hand gently on my stomach, pressing lightly at first, then with a bit more firmness. The sensation was both uncomfortable and oddly surreal, as if the reality of the situation had not yet fully settled into my consciousness.

I winced as he pressed down on a particularly tender spot, his brow furrowing slightly as he concentrated on his task. "You're about three months along, my lady," he said after a moment, his voice calm but tinged with the gravity of the revelation. "The child is developing well, and I can feel the uterus rising above the pubic bone, which is consistent with this stage of pregnancy."

Three months. The words echoed in my mind, a confirmation of what I had feared but could hardly bring myself to believe. Three months—long enough that there was no denying it now, but still early enough that my condition had not yet become obvious to the world.

"How much longer?" I asked, my voice barely a whisper. "How much time do I have before... before it becomes impossible to hide?"

Dr. Turner's expression softened, and he gave a small sigh, clearly understanding the gravity of my question. "It's difficult to say precisely, but I would estimate that within the next month or two, your pregnancy will become more apparent. The uterus will continue to expand, and your abdomen will begin to show. It will be increasingly difficult, if not impossible, to conceal the pregnancy with a corset or clothing."

His words sent a shiver of fear down my spine, the enormity of the situation crashing down on me like a wave. "Is there... is there anything I can do to delay it?" I asked, desperation creeping into my voice.

Dr. Turner hesitated, then shook his head gently. "There are ways to manage your appearance, of course—looser clothing, shawls to drape across your abdomen. But continuing to wear a corset, especially one that is tightly laced, is not advisable. It could cause harm to both you and the child."

The thought of abandoning my corset, the last vestige of control I had over my appearance, filled me with dread. But the physician's words left little room for argument—I could no longer ignore the reality that my body was changing, and soon, the whole world would see it.

I felt Beatrice's hand tighten on mine, her support a lifeline in the midst of my growing panic. "Thank you, Doctor," she said softly, her voice steady despite the fear I knew she must be feeling as well. "We appreciate your honesty."

Dr. Turner gave a small nod, his expression filled with a quiet compassion that only made the situation feel more real. "I understand this is a difficult time, Lady Isabella. I recommend you take care of yourself—eat well, rest as much as you can, and avoid stress as much as possible. Your health, and the health of the child, are of utmost importance."

His words, though well-meaning, felt like the final nail in the coffin of my previous life. The reality of my situation was undeniable now—I was pregnant, and there was no going back.

As Dr. Turner finished the examination and stepped back, I felt a cold numbness settle over me, the full weight of the truth pressing down on my chest. The small, hard mound that had begun to form in my abdomen was no longer something I could dismiss or ignore. It was real, and it was growing, and soon, it would be impossible to hide.

Beatrice helped me dress again, her hands gentle as she fastened the laces of the corset—though this time, she left it looser, mindful of the physician's warning. The familiar pressure was still there, but it felt different now—less like a shield and more like a reminder of the inevitable.

As we left the physician's office and returned to the carriage, the reality of what had just happened began to sink in. The confirmation of my pregnancy felt like a thunderbolt, a jolt of reality that shattered the fragile hope I had clung to that maybe, just maybe, I was mistaken.

But there was no mistake. I was three months pregnant with Cassian's child, and the scandal that had begun as a harmless prank was about to change my life forever.

The ride back to the townhouse was silent, both Beatrice and I lost in our own thoughts. I could feel the weight of the future pressing down on me, the uncertainty of what lay ahead filling me with a sense of dread that I couldn't shake.

When we finally arrived home, Beatrice turned to me, her expression serious but filled with determination. "We need to talk about the next steps, Isabella," she said softly. "This is no longer something we can ignore. We have to decide what to do—how to manage this, and how to protect you."

I nodded, though the enormity of the decisions that lay ahead felt overwhelming. "I know," I whispered, my voice trembling with emotion. "But where do we even begin?"

Beatrice's eyes softened, and she reached out to take my hand, her grip firm and reassuring. "We'll figure it out together," she said, her voice filled with the kind of quiet strength that I had come to rely on. "We'll take it one step at a time. But for now, you need to rest. We'll face this head-on, Isabella, and we'll find a way to get through it."

As I looked into her eyes, I felt a glimmer of hope, a small flicker of strength in the midst of the storm that threatened to overwhelm me. We would face the truth together, and no matter what happened, I knew that I wouldn't have to bear the burden alone.

But as I lay in bed that night, the physician's words echoing in my mind, I couldn't shake the feeling that my life was about to change in ways I couldn't even begin to imagine. The road ahead was uncertain, and the decisions I would have to make in the coming days would shape the rest of my life.

And as I drifted off to sleep, I knew that the time for denial was over. The truth was out, and there was no turning back.

16

Cassian Cavendish

The streets of London had always held a particular charm for me—a blend of elegance and chaos, where the old world met the new, and where one could easily lose themselves in the bustling throngs of society. After several months spent away in the country, attending to family matters that had dragged on far longer than I would have liked, I found myself eager to return to the familiar hum of city life. London was, after all, where I thrived.

As the younger son of the noble Cavendish family, I had always found myself in a peculiar position—close enough to power and wealth to enjoy its benefits, but far enough removed from the burden of responsibility that my older brother, Alexander, bore. It was a position I relished, allowing me the freedom to indulge in my whims and fancies without the weight of expectations that often crushed men of my station.

My return to London was meant to be a quiet one, a reintroduction to the society I had missed during my time away. But as soon as I set foot in the city, it became clear that my absence had done little to dull the ever-turning wheels of gossip. In fact, I was greeted with whispers and sidelong glances from the moment I arrived at my club, and it wasn't long before one of my more talkative acquaintances took it upon himself to fill me in on the latest scandal.

"Cavendish!" Lord Halstead exclaimed, clapping me on the back as I took my seat in the club's lounge. "You've missed quite a stir while you were away. London hasn't been the same without your mischief to keep things interesting."

I grinned, accepting the glass of brandy he handed me. "I'm sure the city has managed to entertain itself in my absence, Halstead. But do tell—what scandal have I missed this time?"

Halstead's eyes gleamed with the thrill of gossip, and he leaned in closer, lowering his voice as if sharing a great secret. "It's Lady Isabella Fairchild," he said, a smirk tugging at the corners of his mouth. "The rumor is that she's pregnant."

I arched an eyebrow, amusement flickering through me at the thought. "Lady Isabella? Pregnant? That's quite the tale."

"It is, isn't it?" Halstead continued, clearly relishing the moment. "They say she announced it herself at one of Lady Evelyn's gatherings, of all places. Can you imagine? The demure and proper Lady Isabella, carrying a child out of wedlock? It's the talk of the town."

I took a sip of my brandy, letting the warmth of the liquor settle in my chest as I considered the information. Lady Isabella Fairchild—a name that had lingered at the edges of my thoughts more often than I cared to admit. Our brief affair had been nothing more than a fleeting indulgence, a moment of passion that we had both agreed was best left in the past. But the memory of that night, of her soft skin beneath my fingers and the fire in her eyes, had stayed with me, even as I had tried to push it aside.

"And what does Lady Isabella have to say about all this?" I asked, my curiosity piqued.

Halstead chuckled, shaking his head. "She's been quiet about the whole thing, from what I've heard. Some say she's denying it, others say she's hiding away. But the rumors are spreading like wildfire, and it seems everyone has their own version of the story."

The thought of Isabella hiding away from the world didn't sit well with me. The Isabella I knew was sharp-witted and fiercely independent, not the sort to be cowed by society's judgment. And yet, the idea of her facing this storm alone stirred something in me—something that I wasn't quite ready to examine too closely.

I leaned back in my chair, a slow smile curling my lips as I considered my next move. "It seems I've returned to London just in time, then. I suppose I'll have to pay Lady Isabella a visit and see if there's any truth to these rumors."

Halstead's eyes widened in surprise, and he let out a low whistle. "You always did have a taste for trouble, Cavendish. But be careful—if the rumors are true, you might find yourself in the middle of a scandal that even you can't charm your way out of."

I laughed, the sound echoing through the lounge. "Oh, Halstead, where's the fun in life without a little scandal? Besides, I've always been rather good at navigating these waters. I'm sure Lady Isabella and I will have plenty to discuss."

But as I left the club that evening, the playful banter with Halstead fading into the background, I couldn't shake the feeling that this situation was more complicated than I had initially thought. The thought of Isabella being pregnant—possibly with my child—was a notion that both intrigued and unsettled me.

The streets of London were busy as ever, carriages rattling by and pedestrians bustling about their evening errands. But as I walked through the familiar throngs, my mind was far from the city's usual distractions. Instead, it kept returning to that night with Isabella, the way we had connected so unexpectedly, the passion that had flared between us like a flame that neither of us had seen coming.

It had been a mistake, we both knew that. From the moment I first laid eyes on Isabella Fairchild, I knew she was different—a woman of grace, intelligence, and wit, qualities that were rare in the glittering circles of London society. Isabella was from a ducal family, her lineage impeccable, her ties to the royal family deep and undeniable. She was destined for greatness, with a future carefully laid out before her. Her path was one of privilege and responsibility, a life of duty that left little room for error.

I, on the other hand, was the younger son of the Cavendish family, a name known more for our charm and rakish tendencies than for our wealth or influence. As the second son, my prospects were limited to the life of a gentleman with no estate to inherit, no title to claim. I was free to enjoy the pleasures of society without the burden of responsibility that weighed so heavily on my elder brother. I reveled in that freedom, embracing it with a reckless abandon that often made me the subject of gossip and speculation.

But despite the differences in our stations, there had been something between us that night—something real. It was a connection that neither of us had expected, something that defied the rigid boundaries of our social roles. When I first approached Isabella at that fateful soirée, I hadn't anticipated anything more than a pleasant conversation. But as the evening wore on, as we found ourselves drawn together in the quiet corners of the room, I realized that this was different. She was different.

We talked for hours, the usual polite small talk quickly giving way to deeper, more meaningful conversation. She spoke of her love for literature, her passion for the arts, and the frustration she felt at the constraints placed upon her by society. I listened, captivated by her every word, and shared my own dreams and fears—the desire for a life that was more than just idle leisure, the struggle to find purpose in a world that expected so little of me.

There was a moment, as we stood by the window, looking out at the city bathed in moonlight, when I felt something shift between us. Her hand brushed against mine, a small, seemingly accidental touch, but it sent a jolt of electricity through me. When I looked into her eyes, I saw the same realization reflected back at me—that this was not just a casual flirtation. There was something more here, something that neither of us had anticipated but both of us felt deeply.

In that moment, I wanted nothing more than to take her in my arms, to kiss her and forget the world outside. But I hesitated, my mind filled with the reality of our situation. Isabella was not just any woman—she was a lady of high standing, with everything to lose. And I... I was just Cassian Cavendish, the inconsequential younger son with little to offer her in return.

But even as those thoughts crossed my mind, I couldn't bring myself to pull away. The connection between us was too strong, the pull too irresistible. And when she looked up at me, her eyes filled with a mix of curiosity and longing, I knew I was lost.

That day, we crossed a line that could never be uncrossed. We met again and again, each time more clandestine than the last, our secret meetings filled with stolen glances and whispered words. We shared sweet moments of laughter and conversation, times when the rest of the world seemed to fade away, leaving only the two of us in a bubble of our own making.

I remember the way her laughter would ring out, clear and bright, whenever I teased her about her love for poetry. Or how she would blush when I caught her stealing a glance at me, her cheeks turning the loveliest shade of pink. There were times when we simply sat in silence, content to be in each other's presence, the unspoken understanding between us more powerful than any words.

But as sweet as those memories were, there was always an undercurrent of insecurity running through them—a nagging doubt that gnawed at the edges of my happiness. I knew that what we were doing was dangerous, that it couldn't last. Isabella had a reputation to uphold, and our relationship, if discovered, would ruin her. She was destined for a life of privilege and duty, and I had no right to jeopardize that.

I often wondered what she saw in me, why she continued to meet me despite the risks. I couldn't offer her the stability or security that she deserved. I had no title, no grand estate, nothing that could compare to the future she was expected to have. I was acutely aware of my own shortcomings, of the fact that I was not the kind of man who could fit into her world.

And yet, I couldn't stay away. There was something about Isabella that drew me in, something that made me want to be better, to be more than what society had deemed me to be. When I was with her, I felt like I was more than just the charming rake everyone knew me as. I felt like I could be the man she needed, the man she deserved.

But as much as I wanted to believe that, there was always a part of me that doubted. The part of me that knew I would never be able to give her the life she was meant to have. The part of me that feared, deep down, that I was only setting us both up for heartbreak.

And then, just as suddenly as it had started, our time together was cut short. I was called away to Birmingham to attend to family business—a textile venture that required my attention. As the second son, my role was to manage the business affairs that my brother, the heir, had little interest in. It was a responsibility I took seriously, though it often kept me away from London for long stretches of time.

I remember the last time I saw her before I left, the way she had looked at me, a mixture of sadness and acceptance in her eyes. We both knew that our affair was nearing its end, that the time had come for us to part ways before we were discovered. But even then, in those final moments, I couldn't bring myself to say goodbye.

We stood in that secluded grove, the sun setting behind the trees, casting long shadows across the grass. I reached out to her, my hand trembling slightly as I brushed a stray curl from her face. "Isabella," I whispered, my voice thick with emotion, "I—"

But the words caught in my throat. I wanted to tell her how much she meant to me, how much I would miss her, but the fear of what those words would mean held me back. Instead, I kissed her—one last, lingering kiss that said everything I couldn't bring myself to voice.

When we finally pulled away, I saw the tears in her eyes, and it took all my strength not to break down in front of her. I pressed one last kiss to her forehead, then turned and walked away, not daring to look back.

I had thought that leaving would make it easier, that the distance would help me forget. But I was wrong. Every day I spent in Birmingham, every letter I didn't write, every moment of silence only served to deepen the ache in my chest. I missed her more than I had ever thought possible, and the thought of her finding someone else, someone more suited to her, filled me with a jealousy I had no right to feel.

And now, if the rumors were true, that something real between us had consequences that neither of us could have foreseen. I had tried to put her out of my mind, to focus on my duties, but the truth was, Isabella had never really left my thoughts. She was always there, just below the surface, a constant reminder of what we had shared—and what we had lost.

I had made a mistake, one that I couldn't take back. And now, we would both have to face the consequences.

17

The Mask of Innocence

The next day, I made my way to the Fairchild residence, my mind swirling with a mix of curiosity and anticipation. The thought of seeing Isabella again, of facing her in the midst of this scandal, filled me with a strange excitement. But beneath that excitement was a thread of concern—concern for her, and for the possible future that lay ahead.

When I arrived at the townhouse, I was greeted by the Fairchilds' butler, who eyed me with a mixture of suspicion and curiosity. "Lord Cavendish," he said with a bow, "to what do we owe the pleasure of your visit?"

"I've come to call on Lady Isabella," I replied smoothly, offering the man my most disarming smile. "Is she at home?"

The butler hesitated for a moment, then nodded. "She is, my lord. I shall inform her of your visit."

As I waited in the grand entrance hall, my gaze wandered over the familiar surroundings, the elegant furnishings and tasteful decor a reminder of the world Isabella inhabited—a world that was so different from my own. But as my thoughts drifted, the sound of footsteps drew my attention, and I turned to see her descending the staircase.

She was as beautiful as I remembered, her dark hair swept up in a simple yet elegant style, her eyes—those sharp, intelligent eyes—fixed on me with an unreadable expression. But there was something different about her, something that made my heart skip a beat. She looked paler than I remembered, and there was a tension in her posture that hadn't been there before.

"Cassian," she greeted me, her voice cool and controlled. "This is a surprise."

"Isabella," I replied with a grin, stepping forward to take her hand. "I couldn't resist the temptation to see you again, especially with all the interesting rumors flying about."

Her eyes flashed with something—irritation, perhaps?—but she quickly masked it, her expression remaining neutral. "I'm sure you've heard all sorts of things," she said lightly, withdrawing her hand from mine. "But I assure you, most of them are just that—rumors."

"And what about the ones that aren't?" I asked, my tone playful but my curiosity genuine.

She hesitated, just for a moment, and in that hesitation, I saw a flicker of something—fear, perhaps, or uncertainty. But then she straightened, her gaze steady as she met mine. "Why don't we sit down?" she suggested, gesturing toward the drawing room. "I'm sure you have plenty of questions."

As we made our way to the drawing room, the air between us was thick with tension, the easy camaraderie we had once shared now overshadowed by the uncertainty of the situation. I could feel the weight of her gaze on me, and I knew that whatever we discussed here would have far-reaching consequences for both of us.

As I sat in the Fairchilds' drawing room, the tension between us was palpable, hanging in the air like a storm cloud about to break. Isabella moved with the same grace I had always admired, her movements controlled and deliberate, as if she were consciously keeping herself in check. The room was bathed in the soft glow of afternoon light filtering through the tall windows, casting delicate shadows across the richly upholstered furniture and ornate rugs. It was a scene of quiet elegance, yet beneath the surface, I could sense the turmoil swirling within her.

Isabella took a seat across from me, her back straight, hands clasped in her lap. For a moment, we simply regarded each other, the silence stretching out as we both gathered our thoughts. I had come here with the intention of uncovering the truth behind the rumors, to confirm or dispel the whispers that had reached every corner of London society. But now that I was here, sitting across from her, I found myself questioning what I truly wanted to discover.

"What is it that you wish to know, Cassian?" she asked, her voice steady but devoid of the warmth it had once held when we were together. There was a guardedness to her that hadn't been there before, as if she were bracing herself for whatever I might say next.

I leaned back in my chair, studying her closely. "Isabella, we've known each other long enough that I can tell when something is weighing on your mind. These rumors... they've caused quite a stir."

Her gaze remained fixed on me, unwavering. "Rumors have a way of doing that, especially in our world. People are always eager to believe the most sensational stories."

"But not all rumors are baseless," I countered gently, hoping to prod her into revealing more. "Some have a kernel of truth to them."

Her lips curved into a faint smile, though it didn't reach her eyes. "And which rumors are you referring to, Cassian? The ones that claim I've been sequestered away with child? Or the ones that suggest I've been secretly married off to some foreign prince?"

She was deflecting, that much was clear. But there was something in the way she spoke, a certain tightness around her mouth, that told me she wasn't entirely unaffected by the gossip swirling around her. The Isabella I knew would have laughed off such absurdities, but this Isabella was different— more cautious, more careful. It made me wonder just how much truth lay beneath the surface.

"I'm referring to the rumors about your condition," I said, choosing my words carefully. "There's talk that you're... expecting."

She stiffened slightly, her knuckles turning white where they gripped the fabric of her gown. It was a small reaction, almost imperceptible, but I noticed it nonetheless. My heart quickened in my chest as I waited for her response.

"Cassian," she began, her tone measured, "I understand that people love to talk, especially when it concerns someone like me. But not every story that's told is true. The idea that I'm with child is nothing more than idle gossip, started by those with nothing better to do."

Her words were firm, her gaze steady, but there was something in her eyes—something fleeting, a shadow of uncertainty—that made me doubt her denial. She was skilled at maintaining her composure, but I had spent enough time with her to know when she was hiding something.

"And you're certain?" I pressed, leaning forward slightly. "There's no truth to it at all?"

She held my gaze for a long moment, and I could see the struggle within her—the desire to keep her secret hidden, balanced against the need to maintain her dignity. But then, as if making a decision, she drew herself up, her expression smoothing into one of polite indifference.

"I can assure you, Cassian," she said with a hint of finality, "that there is no truth to the rumors. I am not pregnant."

It was a clear, unequivocal statement, but something in her tone left me unconvinced. Perhaps it was the way her voice had wavered ever so slightly, or the way her hands fidgeted in her lap, but I couldn't shake the feeling that there was more to this than she was letting on.

Still, I knew better than to push her further. If Isabella had decided to present this story to the world, then that was the version she intended to stick with. And yet, the idea that she might be carrying my child—our child—gnawed at the edges of my mind, refusing to be dismissed so easily.

"Well," I said, leaning back in my chair with a sigh, "I suppose that clears things up, then. I won't press the matter any further."

She offered a small, tight smile, though I could see the relief in her eyes. "Thank you, Cassian. It's best not to give the gossips more fuel for their fires."

We sat in silence for a moment, the tension in the room slowly dissipating as we both adjusted to the new dynamic between us. The easy camaraderie we had once shared was gone, replaced by a delicate balance of guarded politeness and unspoken truths. I couldn't help but feel a pang of regret for the distance that had grown between us—distance created not just by our circumstances, but by the choices we had both made.

"So," she said after a moment, her tone lighter as if trying to steer the conversation into safer waters, "what brings you back to London? I heard you were busy in Birmingham."

I nodded, grateful for the change in topic. "Yes, the family business has kept me occupied. Managing the textile operations is no small feat, especially with the expansion we've been planning."

Her interest seemed genuine, though I could tell it was also a means of avoiding further discussion of the rumors. "And how is the expansion going?"

"Better than expected," I replied, my thoughts momentarily drifting to the stacks of ledgers and contracts waiting for me back at the office. "We're looking at acquiring another mill, which should help us increase production significantly. It's... demanding work, but fulfilling."

Isabella nodded, her expression thoughtful. "It suits you, I think. The work, I mean."

I raised an eyebrow, intrigued by her observation. "You think so?"

She smiled, a real one this time, though still tinged with that elusive sadness. "Yes. You've always been good at finding your way, Cassian. Even when others might have underestimated you."

There was a warmth in her words that took me by surprise, and for a moment, it felt like we were back to how things had been—before the scandal, before the rumors. But as quickly as it came, the moment passed, and the distance between us returned.

I studied her closely, wondering if she felt the same pull of nostalgia, the same longing for what had been. But if she did, she didn't show it. Instead, she rose gracefully from her seat, signaling that our conversation was coming to an end.

"Thank you for visiting, Cassian," she said, her tone polite but dismissive. "It's always a pleasure to see you."

I stood as well, taking her hand in mine once more. "The pleasure is mine, Isabella. And if you ever need anything—anything at all—you know where to find me."

Her eyes softened for just a moment, and I thought I saw a flicker of something in their depths—regret, perhaps, or gratitude. But it was gone before I could be sure, replaced by the carefully constructed mask she had worn throughout our conversation.

"Thank you," she said quietly, her hand slipping out of mine as she took a step back. "I appreciate that."

With a final nod, I turned and made my way to the door, my mind still racing with unanswered questions. The butler reappeared, opening the door for me with a bow, and I stepped out into the cool afternoon air, the weight of our conversation settling heavily on my shoulders.

As I walked away from the Fairchild residence, I couldn't shake the feeling that Isabella was hiding something—something important. But until she was ready to share it, there was little I could do but wait. And waiting had never been my strong suit.

But one thing was certain: the flame that Isabella had ignited was far from extinguished. And something told me that this was only the beginning of a much more complicated game—one that neither of us was prepared for.

As I made my way back to my own residence, I found myself haunted by the memory of her eyes, the way they had lingered on me just a moment too long, the way they had seemed to hold back more than they revealed. And I couldn't help but wonder—what was she really thinking? And how much longer could she keep the truth hidden?

18

A Chance Encounter

The tea party was in full swing by the time I arrived, the scent of roses and fresh pastries mingling with the lively chatter of London's finest. Lady Audley, our hostess for the afternoon, had outdone herself as always, her expansive gardens transformed into a haven of delicate blooms and pristine white linens. The elite of society mingled in clusters, their conversations punctuated by the occasional burst of laughter or the clinking of fine china.

I had attended such gatherings countless times before, and though they were often the perfect breeding grounds for gossip and intrigue, I rarely found them more than mildly entertaining. But today was different. Today, my interest was piqued, not by the usual parade of frivolous conversations, but by the possibility of an unexpected encounter.

As I made my way through the throng of guests, exchanging pleasantries and dodging the occasional probing question about my time away, my eyes scanned the crowd, searching for a particular face. I had no way of knowing if Isabella would be here, but something told me that fate might just decide to play its hand today.

And as luck would have it, I was not disappointed.

I spotted her near one of the elegant marble fountains, standing beside Lady Beatrice and a few other women. She was dressed in a soft lavender gown, the color accentuating her pale complexion and making her look even more ethereal against the backdrop of the garden. But what struck me most was the way she held herself—stiff, almost as if she were bracing herself for something. Her face, though composed, carried an edge of tension that hadn't been there the last time we'd met.

My curiosity deepened as I approached, weaving through the crowd with the practiced ease of someone who had long ago mastered the art of blending into high society while maintaining a careful distance from its more restrictive expectations.

"Lady Isabella," I called out, a smile playing on my lips as I reached her side. "What a pleasant surprise to see you here."

She turned toward me, and for a brief moment, I saw a flicker of something—nervousness, perhaps?—in her eyes before she masked it with a polite smile. "Lord Cavendish," she replied, her tone cordial but not warm. "I didn't expect to see you here."

"I'm full of surprises," I said with a grin, bowing slightly to acknowledge Lady Beatrice and the others before turning my attention back to Isabella. "It seems we've been crossing paths quite a bit lately, haven't we?"

She raised an eyebrow, her expression carefully controlled. "It would seem so. London is a small place, after all."

"Indeed," I agreed, leaning in slightly, lowering my voice just enough to make the conversation feel more intimate. "And in such a small place, it's hard to keep secrets. I'm sure you've noticed how quickly rumors can spread."

Her eyes narrowed slightly, the tension in her posture becoming more pronounced. "Rumors are just that—rumors. They hold no truth unless we give them power."

"Ah, but isn't it fun to wonder where the truth lies?" I teased, watching her closely for any sign that I might be getting under her skin. If I couldn't pry out any information yesterday, then I'll try my luck today. There's no way she'll say I'm boring for repeating the same topic. Isabella will never be able to say that we met privately. "Sometimes, the most scandalous stories have a kernel of truth hidden within them."

For a moment, I thought I saw her composure crack, a flash of something—panic, perhaps?—crossing her features. But she quickly recovered, lifting her chin slightly as she met my gaze head-on.

"Is that what you think, Lord Cavendish?" she asked, her voice steady but tinged with an edge. "That there's truth in every rumor?"

I shrugged, adopting an air of casual indifference, though I could feel the charge in the air between us. "Perhaps. Or perhaps it's simply that rumors are born of curiosity—and curiosity, as we both know, can lead us to uncover all sorts of interesting truths."

Her lips pressed into a thin line, and I could sense that my playful probing was beginning to rattle her. Good. I wanted to see how far I could push her, how long she could maintain that icy composure in the face of the storm brewing within her.

Before she could respond, Lady Beatrice, sensing the rising tension, interjected with a smile. "Lord Cavendish, you always seem to find a way to make any conversation more... lively. But perhaps we should steer clear of such scandalous topics at a tea party, of all places."

I chuckled, inclining my head in acknowledgment. "You're right, Lady Beatrice. I wouldn't want to disrupt the peace with my idle musings."

But as I glanced back at Isabella, I saw that the damage had already been done. Her shoulders were tense, her hands clasped tightly in front of her, as if she were holding herself together by sheer force of will.

"Perhaps I should take a walk," she said suddenly, her voice a touch too bright. "The gardens are lovely this time of year."

Lady Beatrice looked concerned, but she nodded. "Of course, Isabella. I'll join you in a moment."

"I think I'll accompany Lady Isabella," I offered smoothly, ignoring the look of surprise that flashed across Beatrice's face. "It's been too long since I've enjoyed the beauty of Lady Audley's gardens."

Isabella's eyes darted to mine, and I could see the flicker of uncertainty there, but she inclined her head in agreement. "Very well, Lord Cavendish. Shall we?"

I extended my arm to her, and after a moment's hesitation, she took it. As we began to stroll through the manicured paths, the conversation around us faded into the background, leaving us in a bubble of our own making.

For a while, we walked in silence, the tension between us thickening with every step. I could feel her hand trembling slightly against my arm, and I couldn't help but be intrigued by the effect I seemed to have on her. Isabella Fairchild was not a woman easily rattled, and yet, here she was, struggling to maintain her composure.

"You seem different, Isabella," I remarked casually, breaking the silence. "Quieter than usual. I hope I haven't offended you with my teasing."

She glanced at me, her expression unreadable. "I'm not easily offended, Lord Cavendish. But I must admit, I find your interest in these rumors rather... tiresome."

I smiled, but there was no amusement in her tone, only a weariness that hadn't been there before. "Perhaps I'm just curious," I replied lightly. "After all, it's not every day that London is abuzz with talk of a scandal involving someone like you."

Her grip on my arm tightened ever so slightly, and I felt a pang of regret for pushing her so hard. But before I could soften my approach, she spoke, her voice low and filled with a vulnerability I hadn't expected.

"Cassian," she began, using my first name for the first time in our conversation, "you don't know what you're playing with. These rumors... they aren't just idle gossip. They have the power to ruin lives."

I paused, taken aback by the sudden seriousness in her tone. The playful banter between us had taken a turn, and I realized that there was more at stake here than I had anticipated. "Isabella, I—"

She stopped walking, turning to face me with a look of quiet desperation in her eyes. "You think this is all a game, don't you?" she asked, her voice trembling. "You think it's amusing to prod and tease, to see how far you can push me. But this isn't a game, Cassian. This is my life. My reputation. And if these rumors continue to spread... I don't know what will happen."

Her words hit me like a punch to the gut, and for the first time since I'd heard the rumors, I realized the gravity of the situation. This wasn't just another scandal to laugh off or another game to play. This was real. And it was hurting her.

"Isabella," I said softly, my voice full of regret, "I didn't mean to—"

She shook her head, cutting me off. "I know you didn't. But that doesn't change the fact that you did."

The silence that followed was heavy, the air between us charged with unspoken emotions. I had come to this tea party expecting to have a bit of fun, to see how Isabella would react to the rumors swirling around her. But now, standing here with her, I realized that I had crossed a line. A line that could have consequences far more serious than I had imagined.

"I'm sorry," I finally said, the words feeling inadequate but necessary. "I never meant to hurt you, Isabella. I... I didn't realize how serious this was."

She looked at me for a long moment, her eyes searching mine as if trying to decide whether or not to believe me. And then, with a deep breath, she nodded. "Thank you for saying that," she said quietly. "But I need you to understand, Cassian... this isn't something I can just brush off. These rumors... they could destroy me."

I felt a wave of guilt wash over me, the full weight of my actions settling on my shoulders. "I do understand," I said softly. "And I want to help you, Isabella. If there's anything I can do to... to make this right, please tell me."

She hesitated, her eyes softening as she looked at me. "Just... be careful, Cassian," she said after a moment. "Be careful with your words, with your actions. Because once a rumor starts, it's nearly impossible to stop."

I nodded, my chest tightening with a mixture of regret and resolve. "I will," I promised. "I'll be careful. And... if you ever need someone to talk to, or to help you navigate this, I'm here."

Her lips curved into a small, sad smile. "Thank you," she said, her voice barely above a whisper. "That means more to me than you know."

We stood there for a moment longer, the tension between us slowly easing, replaced by a fragile understanding. The playful banter that had once defined our interactions was gone, replaced by something deeper, something more real. And as we turned to continue our walk through the garden, I couldn't shake the feeling that this was just the beginning of something far more complicated than either of us had anticipated.

Isabella Fairchild was no longer just a name or a fleeting memory. She was a woman caught in a web of rumors and scandal, a woman who needed someone to stand by her side. And as I looked at her, I realized that I wanted to be that person, to help her navigate the treacherous waters of London society.

But I also knew that this path would not be an easy one. The rumors were already spreading like wildfire, and the truth—whatever that might be—was bound to come out sooner or later. And when it did, both of our lives would be forever changed.

As we made our way back to the party, the sound of laughter and conversation growing louder with each step, I couldn't help but wonder what the future held for us. Would we find a way to weather this storm together? Or would the rumors and the scandal tear us apart before we even had a chance to truly know each other?

Only time would tell. But one thing was certain: my life, and Isabella's, would never be the same.

19

A Delicate Balance

The days seemed to blur together as I tried to maintain the delicate balance of hiding my pregnancy while navigating the increasingly treacherous waters of London society. The arrival of Cassian back into my life had only added to the pressure, and I found myself constantly on edge, wondering how much longer I could keep up the charade.

At home, I was fortunate to live alone with my brother, Edmund, after our parents had passed away. Edmund was often busy with his work, leaving me to my own devices for much of the day. However, we still shared breakfast and dinner together, and it was during these times that I felt the most vulnerable. Edmund had always been observant, and lately, I had noticed the way his gaze lingered on me, his brow furrowed in suspicion.

"Isabella, you seem... different lately," Edmund remarked one evening as we sat down to dinner. His tone was casual, but I could sense the underlying concern.

I forced a smile, picking up my fork to distract myself from the nerves that tightened in my stomach. "Different? How so, Edmund?"

He studied me for a moment, his eyes narrowing slightly. "You've been quieter than usual. And you've barely touched your food these past few days. Are you feeling unwell?"

The truth was, my appetite had become erratic, swinging from intense cravings to bouts of nausea that made it difficult to eat anything at all. But I couldn't very well tell Edmund that, so I forced another smile and shook my head. "I'm fine, really. Just a bit tired, I suppose. The season has been more taxing than I anticipated."

Edmund didn't look entirely convinced, but he nodded, accepting my explanation for the moment. "If you're sure. Just promise me you'll take care of yourself. I don't want you overexerting yourself."

"I promise," I replied, though the words felt hollow. Taking care of myself had become increasingly difficult as the signs of my pregnancy grew harder to ignore. And the fact that Edmund had started to notice only added to my anxiety.

But it wasn't just Edmund who was growing suspicious. Alice, my loyal maid, had been with me for years, and she knew me better than anyone. It was impossible to hide the changes from her—she was the one who helped me dress each morning, who held back my hair as I suffered through yet another bout of morning sickness, who brought me whatever odd food I happened to be craving at any given moment.

At first, Alice had said nothing, simply doing her job with the quiet efficiency I had always admired. But as the weeks went on and my symptoms became more pronounced, I could sense her growing concern. She never asked any direct questions, but I often caught her watching me with a worried expression, as if she were trying to piece together a puzzle that didn't quite make sense.

The turning point came one morning when I was particularly unwell. The nausea had hit me hard as soon as I woke, and I had barely managed to make it to the basin in time. Alice was by my side in an instant, her hand gentle on my back as she murmured soothing words.

When the sickness finally subsided, I collapsed onto the edge of the bed, utterly exhausted. My head throbbed, and my stomach churned with a mix of hunger and queasiness. I felt weak, fragile—two things I had never wanted to be.

"Alice," I croaked, my voice barely above a whisper. "I... I need to tell you something."

She looked up from where she was fetching a damp cloth, her eyes filled with concern. "Yes, milady?"

I hesitated, the words sticking in my throat. This was not how I had imagined this conversation going, but I knew I couldn't keep this secret from her any longer. She had been too loyal, too caring, and she deserved to know the truth—at least, as much of the truth as I could bear to share. Even if I want to keep my pregnancy a secret, when my belly started to grow, Alice would be the first to notice. So, it's impossible to hide all this any longer. Besides, I could use this unfavorable situation to get Alice to help me.

"I... I'm not just unwell," I began, my hands trembling as I fumbled with the hem of my nightgown. "I'm... I'm with child."

The words hung in the air between us, heavy and undeniable. For a moment, Alice simply stared at me, her eyes wide with shock. Then, slowly, she set the cloth aside and knelt before me, her expression softening into one of quiet understanding.

"Oh, milady," she whispered, her voice filled with sympathy. "I suspected as much, but... I didn't want to pry."

Tears welled up in my eyes, and I felt a wave of relief wash over me. To finally speak the truth, to have someone else share this burden, was more comforting than I could have imagined.

"I'm so sorry, Alice," I said, my voice trembling with emotion. "I didn't mean for this to happen. I... I don't know what to do."

Alice reached out and took my hands in hers, her grip firm and reassuring. "There's no need to apologize, milady. What's done is done, and now we must focus on what comes next."

I nodded, grateful for her pragmatism. "I need your help, Alice. I can't let anyone know—not yet, at least. Edmund... he doesn't know, and I don't want him to find out until I've figured out what to do."

"Of course, milady," Alice said without hesitation. "I'll do whatever I can to help you. But... we'll need to make some adjustments. The corsets you've been wearing... they won't be able to hide the pregnancy for much longer."

I swallowed hard, knowing she was right. The corsets had already begun to feel unbearably tight, and I had been forced to loosen them more and more each day just to be able to breathe. But even that was becoming increasingly difficult as my stomach began to swell, the hard mound beneath my skin growing more prominent with each passing day.

"I don't know what else to do," I admitted, my voice laced with desperation. "If I stop wearing the corsets, it will be obvious. But if I keep wearing them..."

"It could harm you and the child," Alice finished gently. "We'll need to find a compromise, milady. Perhaps we can have the corsets altered, made a bit looser, so they still offer some support without being so restrictive."

I nodded, grateful for her suggestion. "Yes, that might work. But... I'll also need looser dresses. Something that can hide the growing bump."

Alice gave a small smile, her expression determined. "Leave that to me, milady. I'll speak with the dressmaker discreetly, and we'll have some new gowns made up. No one will suspect a thing."

The relief that flooded through me was overwhelming, and I felt a fresh wave of tears spill over. "Thank you, Alice," I whispered, my voice choked with emotion. "I don't know what I'd do without you."

She squeezed my hands gently, her eyes filled with a quiet strength that I desperately needed. "You won't have to find out, milady. We'll get through this together."

As Alice helped me dress that morning, her movements careful and considerate, I couldn't help but feel a deep sense of gratitude for her loyalty. She had been with me through thick and thin, and now, in the midst of this crisis, she was proving once again just how invaluable she was.

But even as I took comfort in Alice's support, I knew that the road ahead was fraught with challenges. Hiding my pregnancy from Edmund, from society, from Cassian... it was a task that seemed nearly impossible. And yet, I had no choice but to try.

As I stepped into the newly loosened corset, the fabric no longer digging painfully into my stomach, I couldn't shake the feeling that time was running out. The changes in my body were becoming harder to ignore, and I knew that it was only a matter of time before someone else noticed—someone who wouldn't be as understanding as Alice.

And when that day came, the carefully constructed facade I had built would come crashing down, leaving me exposed and vulnerable in a world that had little mercy for women in my situation.

But for now, I had to focus on the present, on each day as it came. I had to be strong, to hold onto the hope that somehow, some way, I would find a way through this.

Because if there was one thing I had learned in my time navigating London society, it was that survival was often a matter of wit and willpower. And I had both in spades.

20

The Pressure Mounts

London was a city built on whispers, on the quiet exchange of secrets and the sharp edges of gossip that cut deeper than any blade. It was a game, a dance, one that I had always played with a certain detached amusement. But as I moved through the city in those days, there was a growing sense of unease that I couldn't quite shake—a feeling that the rules of the game were shifting, and that this time, the stakes were far higher than I had anticipated.

The rumors about Isabella had reached a fever pitch. What had started as idle speculation among the ton had snowballed into something much more insidious, something that seemed to cling to the very air we breathed. Everywhere I went, I heard her name, accompanied by hushed tones and knowing glances, as if the entire city were in on a secret that I had yet to fully uncover.

It was infuriating.

Isabella Fairchild was no stranger to society's scrutiny—none of us were. But this... this was different. There was a cruelty to it, a viciousness that made me bristle with anger every time I heard someone speak of her with that particular brand of smug satisfaction that only the truly self-righteous could muster.

And yet, despite my growing irritation, there was also something else— something that gnawed at the edges of my thoughts, refusing to be ignored.

I couldn't quite put my finger on it, but I knew that something was wrong. Very wrong.

Isabella had always been a master of composure, a woman who could navigate the treacherous waters of London society with grace and poise. But in our recent encounters, I had seen cracks in that facade, small but unmistakable signs that she was struggling to maintain her usual control.

It was in the way her smile didn't quite reach her eyes, in the slight tremor in her hands when she thought no one was looking. It was in the way she seemed to avoid certain topics, deflecting my questions with a quick wit that, while impressive, only served to heighten my suspicions.

I didn't like it.

More than that, I didn't like the way the rest of society had begun to treat her. The change was subtle at first, almost imperceptible, but as the rumors continued to swirl, it became more pronounced. Invitations that once arrived with clockwork regularity began to dwindle, and when she did attend events, I noticed the way people would whisper behind their fans, their eyes following her with a mixture of curiosity and something darker—judgment, perhaps, or pity.

Isabella had always been a bright light in any room, her presence commanding attention not because she demanded it, but because it was simply impossible to ignore. But now, that light was dimming, overshadowed by the relentless tide of gossip that threatened to pull her under.

And it was driving me mad.

I had always prided myself on my ability to remain detached, to view the machinations of society with a certain level of amusement. But this... this was different. I couldn't stand by and watch as Isabella was torn apart by rumors that might very well be baseless. And if they weren't... well, that was something I needed to know, too.

I had to find out the truth.

The decision settled over me with a clarity that surprised me. I had been content to play the role of the charming rake, toying with Isabella's nerves and enjoying our verbal sparring matches. But now, I realized that there was more at stake than just a game of wits. There was something deeper here, something that I couldn't ignore any longer.

I needed to see her, to talk to her—to understand what was really going on behind those carefully guarded eyes.

The opportunity came sooner than I expected.

It was a crisp autumn afternoon, the kind of day that made London almost bearable, with the chill in the air serving as a reminder that the season was changing. I had spent the morning at my club, half-listening to the conversations around me, my thoughts continually drifting back to Isabella. The more I thought about it, the more convinced I became that I needed to confront her, to force her to tell me the truth.

And so, when I learned that she would be attending a small gathering at Lady Ainsley's that afternoon, I knew it was the perfect opportunity. I left the club with a renewed sense of purpose, my mind racing with the questions I needed answers to.

When I arrived at Lady Ainsley's townhouse, the gathering was already in full swing. It was a small affair, more intimate than the grand balls and soirées that usually defined the season. As I entered the drawing room, I immediately spotted Isabella across the room, engaged in conversation with a few other ladies. She looked as composed as ever, her smile polite, her posture perfect. But as I watched her, I could see the tension in her shoulders, the way her eyes seemed to flicker with something like anxiety.

I made my way toward her, weaving through the clusters of guests with a casual ease that belied the turmoil brewing inside me. When I finally reached her, she looked up, her eyes widening slightly in surprise.

"Cassian," she greeted me, her voice as steady as ever. "I didn't expect to see you here."

"I could say the same," I replied, offering her a charming smile. "But I suppose fate has a way of bringing us together, doesn't it?"

She tilted her head slightly, her eyes narrowing in suspicion. "What do you want, Cassian?"

Her directness caught me off guard, but I quickly recovered, leaning in slightly to lower my voice. "I want to talk, Isabella. Alone."

She hesitated, glancing around the room as if searching for an escape. But there was no way out, and she knew it. With a resigned sigh, she nodded. "Very well. There's a balcony just off the drawing room. We can speak there."

I followed her out of the crowded room and onto the balcony, where the cool air was a welcome relief from the stuffy atmosphere inside. The city stretched out before us, the sounds of carriages and distant conversations providing a backdrop to the tension between us.

Isabella turned to face me, her expression guarded. "What is it, Cassian? What do you want to talk about?"

I studied her for a moment, taking in the slight pallor of her skin, the way her hands fidgeted with the fabric of her dress. She was nervous—something I had never seen in her before. It only strengthened my resolve.

"I want to know the truth, Isabella," I said, my voice firm. "About the rumors. About what's really going on."

She stiffened, her eyes flashing with something like anger. "I told you before, Cassian. Rumors are just that—rumors. There's nothing to them."

I shook my head, taking a step closer. "I don't believe you. And I think you know that I won't stop until I get to the bottom of this."

She turned away from me, her gaze fixed on the city below. "Why do you care, Cassian? Why does it matter to you?"

Her question caught me off guard, and for a moment, I didn't have an answer. Why did I care? Why did it matter so much to me?

But as I looked at her, standing there with her back to me, I realized the truth—the truth that I had been avoiding for far too long.

"Because it's you, Isabella," I said quietly, the words slipping out before I could stop them. "Because it's you, and I can't stand the thought of you going through this alone."

She turned to face me again, her eyes wide with surprise. For a moment, we simply stared at each other, the silence between us heavy with unspoken emotions.

"I'm not alone," she finally said, her voice barely above a whisper. "I have Alice. I have Beatrice."

"But they're not me," I replied, taking another step closer. "And you know that."

Her gaze dropped to the ground, her hands twisting together in front of her. "I can't tell you, Cassian. I just... I can't."

The vulnerability in her voice tugged at something deep inside me, and I reached out, gently taking her hand in mine. "You can, Isabella. Whatever it is, you can tell me. We'll figure it out together."

She looked up at me, her eyes filled with a mixture of fear and something else—something that looked almost like hope. But before she could say anything, the door to the balcony opened, and Lady Ainsley stepped out, her expression one of polite curiosity.

"Lord Cavendish, Lady Isabella," she said with a smile. "I was just coming to see if you needed anything."

Isabella quickly pulled her hand from mine, her composure snapping back into place like a well-worn mask. "No, thank you, Lady Ainsley. We were just finishing our conversation."

Lady Ainsley nodded, her smile never wavering. "Of course. Please, do come back inside when you're ready."

As she disappeared back into the drawing room, Isabella turned to me, her eyes pleading. "Please, Cassian. Let it go."

But I couldn't. Not now. Not when I was so close to the truth.

"Isabella," I began, but she shook her head, cutting me off.

"Not here," she whispered, her voice urgent. "Please."

I hesitated, then nodded, stepping back to give her the space she so clearly needed. "All right. But this isn't over, Isabella. We're going to talk about this. Soon."

She didn't respond, simply turned and walked back inside, leaving me alone on the balcony with nothing but the sound of the city and the weight of my unresolved questions.

As I stood there, the cool breeze brushing against my face, I knew one thing for certain: I wouldn't rest until I had the truth. And whatever that truth was, I would be there for Isabella—whether she wanted me to be or not.

21

A Tense Dinner Party

The atmosphere in Lady Ainsley's townhouse had shifted as the day turned to night, the gentle murmur of conversation giving way to the more formal and subdued tones of a dinner party. The long dining table was set with the finest china and gleaming silverware, the soft glow of candlelight casting flickering shadows on the faces of the guests. It was the kind of evening where one's every word and gesture was observed, dissected, and discussed by those who prided themselves on their social acumen.

I had been looking forward to the dinner, though now, seated beside Isabella, I found the anticipation tinged with a different kind of tension. The conversation on the balcony earlier had left me with more questions than answers, and as the evening progressed, I found myself watching her with a heightened sense of awareness, searching for any sign that might betray the truth she was so determined to keep hidden.

Isabella, for her part, was doing her best to maintain her composure, but I could see the strain in her eyes, the way she avoided my gaze, focusing instead on her plate or on the conversation flowing around us. She was usually so adept at navigating these social situations, but tonight, there was a brittleness to her that I hadn't seen before—a fragility that made me even more determined to uncover what she was hiding.

The first course was served, and as the plates were set before us, I leaned slightly closer to her, keeping my voice low so as not to draw the attention of the other guests. "You seemed a bit flustered earlier, Isabella," I remarked casually, my tone light despite the weight of the question beneath it. "I hope I didn't upset you."

She tensed at my words, her fingers tightening around her fork. "Not at all, Cassian," she replied, her voice smooth but lacking its usual warmth. "It was just... an unexpected conversation."

"Unexpected?" I echoed, my curiosity piqued. "How so?"

She glanced at me briefly before turning her attention back to her plate, cutting into the delicate piece of fish with a precision that belied the tension in her movements. "I wasn't expecting you to be so... inquisitive," she said, her tone carefully neutral. "You're usually content to leave well enough alone."

I smiled, though the expression felt more like a mask than anything else. "Perhaps I've changed," I suggested, watching her closely for any reaction. "Or perhaps there's something about this situation that makes me want to dig a little deeper."

Her hand stilled for just a moment before she resumed eating, her movements a fraction more deliberate than before. "There's nothing to dig into, Cassian," she said quietly. "The rumors are just that—rumors. They'll pass, as they always do."

"Perhaps," I allowed, leaning back slightly in my chair. "But something tells me that this time, it's not that simple."

She didn't respond, her gaze fixed on her plate as she continued to eat in silence. I could see the way her shoulders were drawn tight, the way her breath seemed to catch ever so slightly with each word she spoke. It was subtle, but I had spent enough time with her to notice the difference—the way she was holding herself together with sheer force of will.

The second course was served, and the conversation around the table shifted to lighter topics—travel, fashion, the latest plays in the West End. I participated when necessary, offering the occasional comment or laugh, but my attention remained focused on Isabella. She was trying so hard to maintain her composure, but I could see the cracks forming, the way her mask was beginning to slip.

As the main course was brought out—an elaborate dish of roasted pheasant with a rich, savory sauce—I decided to try a different approach. I leaned in again, keeping my tone casual but pointed. "You know, Isabella, I've always admired your ability to handle anything society throws your way. It's one of the things that makes you so remarkable."

She looked up at me, her expression guarded. "Flattery, Cassian? I didn't think that was your style."

"It's not flattery if it's true," I countered with a small smile. "But even the strongest of us can falter under enough pressure. And I can't help but wonder... is that what's happening here?"

She set her fork down with a deliberate care, her fingers trembling slightly as she reached for her glass of wine. I could see the way her chest rose and fell with each shallow breath, the way she seemed to be struggling to maintain her composure.

"Cassian," she began, her voice low and strained, "please, just... let it go. Whatever you think you know, whatever you're trying to uncover... it's better if you don't."

There was a pleading note in her voice that I hadn't expected, and it only served to deepen my concern. Whatever this was, it was more serious than I had initially thought. I had expected a bit of intrigue, perhaps a scandalous secret, but this... this felt different. This felt like something that could truly hurt her.

"I can't do that, Isabella," I said softly, my voice filled with a sincerity that I hoped would reach her. "Not when I can see how much this is affecting you. You don't have to go through this alone, whatever it is."

Her eyes met mine then, and I saw the fear in them—the fear she had been trying so hard to hide. It was a fleeting moment, a crack in the armor she had built around herself, but it was enough. Enough for me to see that whatever she was dealing with, it was tearing her apart from the inside.

Before she could respond, the sound of a spoon tapping against a glass rang out, signaling the start of a toast. Lord Ainsley, ever the gracious host, rose to his feet, raising his glass with a broad smile.

"To friends, old and new," he declared, his voice carrying across the table. "May we continue to find joy in each other's company and weather the storms of life with grace and dignity."

The guests raised their glasses in response, the clinking of crystal filling the room. I lifted my own glass, but my mind was far from the toast. I was still focused on Isabella, on the way she seemed to withdraw into herself, her face a mask of calm even as her hands trembled slightly around the stem of her glass.

As the evening wore on, the tension between us only grew, a silent battle that neither of us seemed willing to concede. Every word, every glance was loaded with meaning, the unspoken questions hanging heavy in the air between us.

By the time dessert was served—a delicate confection of layered cream and berries—I could see the strain beginning to take its toll on her. She barely touched her dessert, her usual appetite replaced by a sense of unease that was impossible to ignore. Her face was pale, her lips pressed into a thin line as she struggled to maintain her composure.

I knew then that I couldn't keep pushing her, not tonight. Whatever she was hiding, it was causing her more distress than I had realized, and the last thing I wanted was to be the one who pushed her over the edge.

As the dinner drew to a close and the guests began to take their leave, I stood and offered her my arm, a gesture that felt strangely formal given the tension between us. "Shall I escort you to your carriage, Lady Isabella?" I asked, my voice gentler now, lacking the edge it had carried throughout the evening.

She hesitated for a moment before nodding, her hand resting lightly on my arm as I led her out of the dining room and toward the front door. The cool night air was a welcome relief as we stepped outside, the chill brushing against my skin and clearing some of the fog that had settled over my thoughts.

Isabella was quiet as we walked, her gaze fixed on the ground in front of us. I could feel the tension radiating from her, the way she seemed to be holding herself together by the thinnest of threads. When we reached her carriage, I turned to face her, my hand still resting on her arm.

"Isabella," I said softly, my voice filled with the concern I had been trying to keep at bay, "whatever this is, whatever you're going through... you don't have to do it alone. Let me help you."

For a moment, she looked up at me, her eyes filled with a mixture of fear, sadness, and something else—something I couldn't quite place. But then she shook her head, her expression hardening as she withdrew her hand from mine.

"Thank you, Cassian," she said quietly, her voice steady once more. "But this is something I have to handle on my own."

I wanted to argue, to tell her that she didn't have to shoulder this burden alone, but the look in her eyes stopped me. She was resolved, determined to face whatever this was on her own terms. And as much as I hated it, I knew that I had to respect that.

"Very well," I said, taking a step back. "But know that I'm here if you need me. Anytime."

She nodded, her lips curving into a faint, bittersweet smile. "Goodnight, Cassian."

"Goodnight, Isabella," I replied, watching as she stepped into her carriage and disappeared into the night.

I just wanted to hug her and tell her that I was ready to do anything. However, in the end I just stared at her as she walked away. I guess I had to wait until Isabella really opened up to me or I had to find another way for her to talk to me.

As I stood there, alone in the cool evening air, I couldn't shake the feeling that I was missing something—some crucial piece of the puzzle that would make everything make sense. But whatever it was, Isabella wasn't ready to share it with me.

And that, more than anything, made me worry.

22

An Unexpected Meeting

The invitation arrived the next morning, delivered by a footman with impeccable timing as I was finishing my breakfast. The envelope was plain, unassuming, with no hint of the significance it carried. But as I took it from the tray and unfolded the crisp paper, my heart sank.

Isabella, the note began, the familiar script instantly recognizable as Cassian's. *I find myself in need of your counsel regarding a matter concerning a mutual acquaintance. Would you be so kind as to meet me at Hyde Park at your earliest convenience? Your insight would be invaluable.*

There was nothing overtly alarming about the note, but the understated tone, coupled with Cassian's recent behavior, set my nerves on edge. This wasn't just a casual request there was something more beneath the surface, something he wasn't saying. And as I read the note again, my heart began to race.

I had been expecting this—dreading it, even. The tension between us had been building steadily since that dinner party at Lady Ainsley's, and I knew it was only a matter of time before Cassian sought me out, determined to pry the truth from my lips. I had managed to hold him at bay so far, but I wasn't sure how much longer I could keep up the charade.

The morning passed in a blur of nervous anticipation. I tried to distract myself with the usual routine—reading, embroidering, anything to keep my mind occupied—but the thought of meeting Cassian lingered, a persistent knot of anxiety in my chest. I knew I couldn't avoid him forever, but the idea of facing him, of potentially having to confess the truth, filled me with a deep, gnawing dread.

By the time I arrived at Hyde Park, the sun had climbed higher in the sky, casting dappled shadows through the trees. The park was bustling with activity—families out for a stroll, couples enjoying the fine weather—but I felt strangely detached from it all, as if I were moving through a dream.

I spotted Cassian near the Serpentine, standing by the water's edge with his hands clasped behind his back. He was dressed impeccably, as always, his posture relaxed, yet there was an air of quiet intensity about him that set my heart pounding. He turned as I approached, his expression unreadable, but his eyes—those sharp, piercing eyes—held a look that made me want to turn and flee.

"Isabella," he greeted me, his voice smooth but tinged with something I couldn't quite place. "Thank you for meeting me on such short notice."

"Of course," I replied, forcing a smile as I tried to steady my breathing. "What's this about, Cassian? You mentioned a mutual acquaintance?"

He waved a hand dismissively, a small smile playing on his lips. "I admit, that was merely a pretense to get you here. I didn't think you would agree to meet if I had been completely honest about my intentions."

I felt a pang of irritation at his confession, but I quickly tamped it down, knowing that any display of emotion would only play into his hands. "What do you want, Cassian?" I asked, my tone sharper than I intended.

His smile faded, replaced by a look of quiet concern. "I wanted to see you, Isabella. To talk. I've been worried about you."

"Worried?" I echoed, forcing a laugh that sounded hollow even to my own ears. "There's no need to worry about me. I'm perfectly fine."

He took a step closer, his gaze never leaving mine. "I don't believe you. You haven't been yourself lately, Isabella. You're... different. And I can't help but feel that there's something you're not telling me."

The intensity in his voice sent a shiver down my spine, and I turned away, focusing on the water to avoid his penetrating gaze. "You're imagining things, Cassian," I said, my voice trembling slightly despite my efforts to keep it steady. "There's nothing wrong."

"Isabella," he said softly, and I felt his hand gently touch my arm, a gesture that was both comforting and unsettling. "You don't have to lie to me. I know something is wrong. I can see it in your eyes, in the way you carry yourself. You're not alone, whatever this is. You can trust me."

The sincerity in his voice was almost too much to bear, and I felt a wave of emotion rise up within me, threatening to break through the carefully constructed facade I had maintained for so long. But I couldn't afford to let my guard down, not now, not when everything was at stake.

I pulled away from his touch, wrapping my arms around myself as if to ward off the chill that had settled in my bones. "You don't know what you're talking about, Cassian," I said, my voice brittle. "There's nothing to trust you with. I'm fine. Everything is fine."

"Isabella, please," he pressed, his tone urgent now. "I'm not trying to pry, but I care about you. I can see that you're struggling, and it's killing me to watch you go through this alone. Whatever it is, whatever you're hiding—I can help you. Just tell me the truth."

The dam I had built around my emotions was beginning to crack, and I could feel the tears welling up in my eyes, threatening to spill over. I had kept the secret for so long, borne the burden in silence, and now, with Cassian standing before me, offering his support, I felt the overwhelming urge to finally let it all out—to confess the truth and relieve myself of the crushing weight that had been pressing down on me.

But I couldn't. I couldn't let him in, couldn't allow him to see the full extent of my vulnerability. It was too dangerous, too risky. If he knew the truth, it would change everything—between us, between me and the rest of society. I had worked so hard to keep up the facade, to protect myself from the judgment and scorn that would inevitably follow if the truth were revealed.

"I can't," I whispered, my voice breaking as I turned away from him, blinking back the tears that blurred my vision. "I can't tell you, Cassian. Please, just... let it go."

For a moment, there was silence between us, the tension thick and suffocating. I could feel his eyes on me, could sense the frustration and concern radiating from him. But he didn't press me further, didn't push me to confess what I wasn't ready to reveal.

Instead, he took a step back, his voice quiet but filled with determination. "All right, Isabella. I won't force you to tell me. But I want you to know that I'm here for you, no matter what. Whenever you're ready, whenever you need me—I'll be here."

His words, so sincere and full of promise, only made the ache in my chest deepen. I wanted so badly to believe him, to trust in the comfort and support he offered. But the fear, the uncertainty, held me back, keeping me locked in the prison of my own making.

"Thank you, Cassian," I said softly, my voice barely audible as I turned to face him once more. "But some things... some things are better left unsaid."

He studied me for a long moment, his expression unreadable. Then, with a small nod, he took a step back, giving me the space I so desperately needed. "Very well," he said quietly. "But remember what I said, Isabella. I'm here for you, whenever you're ready."

I nodded, unable to find the words to respond. The moment between us felt heavy with unspoken emotions, with the weight of all the things we had left unsaid. I could see the concern in his eyes, the frustration at being kept at arm's length, and it only made the guilt in my heart grow stronger.

As the silence stretched on, I knew I couldn't stay any longer. I needed to get away, to be alone with my thoughts before I broke down completely. "I should go," I murmured, my voice trembling. "Thank you for the meeting, Cassian."

He didn't try to stop me as I turned and began to walk away, my footsteps heavy on the gravel path. But I could feel his gaze on me, could sense the turmoil in his heart as I left him standing there by the water, the distance between us growing with each step.

As I walked through the park, my emotions in turmoil, I couldn't help but wonder if I had made a mistake. Maybe I should have told him the truth, confided in him as he had asked. But the fear, the uncertainty, was too great. The risk of exposing my secret, of letting someone else in, was too much to bear.

For now, I would continue to carry the burden alone, to keep up the facade that had become my only shield against the world. But as I walked away from Cassian, I couldn't shake the feeling that I was losing something precious—something I might never be able to reclaim.

And as the tears finally spilled over, I knew that the truth, no matter how much I tried to hide it, would eventually come to light. And when it did, I would have to face the consequences, whatever they might be.

But for now, I could only keep walking, the weight of my secret growing heavier with each passing moment.

23

Conflicted Hearts

The walk back from Hyde Park felt longer than usual, each step weighed down by the thoughts swirling in my mind. The city around me seemed distant, muffled, as if I were moving through a fog. The sounds of bustling carriages, the chatter of passersby, even the birds singing in the trees—all of it faded into the background, drowned out by the turmoil inside my head.

Cassian's words echoed in my ears, replaying over and over like a haunting melody. *"I'm here for you, whenever you're ready."* Such simple words, and yet they carried a weight that I couldn't ignore. He had always been charming, playful, someone who could flirt and banter with the best of them, but today, there had been something different in his tone—something deeper, more sincere. And that sincerity had shaken me in ways I wasn't prepared to face.

I had always been careful with my emotions, guarding them closely, especially when it came to men like Cassian. He was the type who could easily steal your heart with a well-placed compliment, only to leave you in ruins when he moved on to the next conquest. I had promised myself I wouldn't fall for his charms, that I would keep our interactions light and meaningless.

But now, as I walked through the crowded streets, I realized that it wasn't that simple. My feelings for Cassian were far more complicated than I had ever admitted, even to myself.

I had tried to convince myself that our brief affair had been nothing more than a momentary lapse in judgment, a fleeting passion that would fade with time. But time had passed, and instead of fading, my feelings had only grown stronger, more tangled, until I could no longer ignore them.

Cassian was different from other men. He had a way of seeing through the masks people wore, of cutting through the pretense and reaching the truth hidden beneath. It was both exhilarating and terrifying, especially for someone like me, who had spent so long building walls around my heart.

And yet, despite my best efforts, those walls were beginning to crumble.

As I reached the steps of my townhouse, I paused, my hand resting on the cool stone railing. The weight of my secret pressed heavily on my chest, making it difficult to breathe. I knew that I couldn't keep this up much longer—the lies, the deception, the constant fear of being discovered. It was all becoming too much to bear.

But the thought of telling Cassian the truth, of seeing the look of shock or, worse, disappointment on his face, filled me with dread. What would he think of me? Would he see me as weak, as someone who had failed to live up to the standards society expected of a woman in my position? Or would he be angry, feeling betrayed by the fact that I had kept something so important from him?

And what if... what if he didn't care at all? What if he walked away, leaving me to deal with the consequences on my own?

That was the thought that frightened me the most. The idea of facing this alone, without Cassian's support, was unbearable. But at the same time, I couldn't bring myself to risk everything by telling him the truth.

I took a deep breath, trying to steady myself as I entered the house. The familiar scent of lavender and polished wood greeted me, a reminder of the life I had built for myself—a life that was now on the brink of unraveling. I needed time to think, to sort through my feelings and figure out what to do next. But time was running out, and I knew it.

As I made my way upstairs to my chambers, I couldn't shake the image of Cassian's face from my mind—the concern in his eyes, the softness in his voice as he told me he was there for me. He had always been confident, almost arrogant, in the way he carried himself, but today, there had been a vulnerability in him that I hadn't seen before. It was as if he truly cared, not just about the rumors or the scandal, but about me.

The thought sent a shiver down my spine, a mix of fear and longing that left me feeling more conflicted than ever. I had always prided myself on my independence, on my ability to handle whatever life threw at me. But now, for the first time, I found myself wanting something more—wanting someone to stand by my side, to share the burden I had been carrying alone for so long.

But could I trust Cassian with that? Could I trust him with the truth, with the most vulnerable parts of myself, knowing that it might change everything between us?

I reached my chambers and closed the door behind me, leaning against it as I let out a shaky breath. The room was quiet, the afternoon light filtering through the curtains, casting soft shadows on the floor. It was a familiar, comforting space, but today, it felt suffocating, the walls closing in around me as the weight of my thoughts pressed down on me.

I moved to the window and looked out at the garden below, the flowers blooming in a riot of colors, a stark contrast to the turmoil in my heart. I had always found solace in the garden, in the simple beauty of nature, but today, even that couldn't ease the ache in my chest.

Cassian's face appeared in my mind again, and I felt a pang of longing that I couldn't deny. I wanted to tell him the truth, to share the burden with someone who might understand. But the fear held me back, the fear of what his reaction might be, the fear of losing him altogether.

I sighed, running a hand through my hair as I tried to make sense of it all. How had things become so complicated? How had a simple, playful affair turned into something so tangled and messy?

And why, despite everything, did I still find myself drawn to him, still wanting to be near him, even as the fear of what might happen if he knew the truth gnawed at me?

The questions circled in my mind, with no clear answers in sight. I knew I couldn't keep this up much longer—the secrecy, the constant lying to myself and others. But the thought of letting Cassian in, of trusting him with the truth, terrified me more than I cared to admit.

I turned away from the window, pacing the length of the room as I tried to think. What was I supposed to do? How could I navigate this without losing everything I had worked so hard to protect?

And then, almost as if in answer to my thoughts, a memory surfaced—a memory of the day Cassian and I had shared, the day that had led to all of this. It had been a day of passion, of intense emotion, but also of connection. We had talked for hours, sharing our thoughts and fears in a way that felt more intimate than anything physical. It had been a moment of vulnerability, of trust.

And now, as I stood alone in my room, I realized that the connection I had felt that night hadn't disappeared. It was still there, lingering beneath the surface, waiting for me to acknowledge it.

Maybe... maybe I could trust him. Maybe, just maybe, he would understand

But even as the thought crossed my mind, the fear rose up again, choking off any hope before it could take root. The consequences of telling him the truth were too great, too risky. I couldn't afford to lose him, not now, not when I needed him the most.

I sank down onto the edge of the bed, my head in my hands as the tears finally came, hot and relentless. I had spent so long trying to be strong, trying to keep everything together, but now, I felt like I was falling apart, the pieces of my carefully constructed life crumbling around me.

And through it all, one thought kept repeating in my mind, over and over: *What if I tell him? What if I tell him, and he walks away?*

It was a question that had no easy answer, a question that left me paralyzed with fear.

But beneath that fear, beneath the uncertainty, there was something else—something that I couldn't quite name, but that I knew was there, waiting for me to acknowledge it.

It was the hope that maybe, just maybe, Cassian wouldn't walk away. That maybe he would stay, that he would be the one person who could help me carry this burden, who could understand what I was going through.

But that hope was fragile, easily crushed by the weight of my fear. And until I could find the courage to face that fear, to take the risk of trusting him with the truth, I knew that I would remain trapped in this web of lies and secrecy, alone and uncertain of what the future held.

And as the tears continued to fall, I realized that I was no closer to an answer than I had been before. The conflict in my heart remained, unresolved and agonizing, a constant reminder of the choice that lay before me—a choice that I wasn't sure I was strong enough to make.

24

The Unveiling

The morning began like any other, the sunlight streaming through the curtains, bathing the room in a soft, golden glow that belied the storm brewing within me. For weeks, I had managed to maintain my facade, concealing the truth from everyone, including my brother, Edmund. But deep down, I knew that my time was running out. The signs of my pregnancy were becoming harder to hide, and each day brought a new wave of anxiety that threatened to pull me under.

I had become adept at avoiding Edmund's scrutiny, timing my appearances to when I knew he would be occupied, slipping away before he had a chance to notice the subtle changes in my appearance. But today, it seemed, my luck had run out.

It was during breakfast—a routine meal that we had shared countless times—that everything came crashing down.

Edmund had been quiet that morning, more so than usual. He sat at the head of the table, his eyes fixed on the newspaper in front of him, the tension in his posture betraying the calm he tried to project. I could feel his gaze flicker toward me every now and then, a silent pressure that made my pulse quicken with each passing moment.

I had dressed carefully, choosing a gown with a high waistline that did its best to disguise the growing swell of my stomach. But as I sat across from Edmund, I could feel his eyes on me, his scrutiny more intense than it had ever been before.

The silence between us stretched on, heavy and suffocating. I focused on my plate, forcing myself to take small bites of the food that now felt like lead in my mouth. My appetite had waned in recent weeks, the constant nausea making it difficult to enjoy even the simplest of meals. But I couldn't afford to draw attention to myself by leaving the food untouched.

Edmund's gaze was burning into me, and I could feel the weight of it pressing down on me like a physical force. I tried to keep my composure, to act as if everything was perfectly normal, but inside, I was a whirlwind of nerves.

The footman approached with a tureen of soup, and I welcomed the distraction. I reached out to take the ladle, my hands trembling slightly as I served myself. But the moment my hand touched the spoon, a wave of dizziness washed over me. My vision blurred, and before I could steady myself, the ladle slipped from my grasp.

The soup spilled across the table, splashing onto my dress. I gasped, instinctively jumping up from my chair, my hands frantically brushing at the hot liquid soaking into the fabric. But as I stood, my movements frantic, the fabric of my gown clung to my body, revealing the unmistakable curve of my belly.

The room seemed to freeze around me. I could feel Edmund's eyes on me, sharp and penetrating, as if he were seeing me—truly seeing me—for the first time in weeks. The truth, which I had so carefully hidden, was now laid bare for him to see.

"Isabella," Edmund's voice was low, but it cut through the silence like a knife. "What is this?"

My heart pounded in my chest, my breath coming in short, panicked gasps. I opened my mouth to speak, but no words came out. The tears that I had held back for so long began to well up in my eyes, blurring my vision as I looked at my brother.

He stood from his chair, his expression a mix of confusion, anger, and concern. "Isabella," he said again, his tone more urgent this time. "What are you hiding from me?"

I couldn't do it. I couldn't bring myself to admit the truth, to see the disappointment in his eyes. But the truth was no longer something I could keep hidden. The evidence was right there, plain for him to see, and there was no escaping it.

As I stood there, trembling and soaked in the spilled soup, I felt the dam I had built around my emotions begin to crack. The weight of the secret I had been carrying for weeks was too much to bear, and the realization that I could no longer hide it from Edmund broke something inside me.

The tears spilled over, running down my cheeks as I tried to stammer out an explanation. "Edmund... I... I didn't mean for this to happen..."

He moved toward me, his face a mask of barely controlled emotion. "Isabella," he said, his voice tight with concern, "are you... are you pregnant?"

The words hung in the air between us, heavy and suffocating. I couldn't bring myself to answer, the sobs rising in my throat, choking me as I stood there, frozen in place.

Edmund's expression shifted, the anger fading as he took in the sight of me—disheveled, tear-streaked, and utterly broken. His shoulders slumped, the tension draining out of him as he realized the full extent of what was happening.

"Oh, Isabella," he murmured, his voice softening with a mix of sadness and disbelief. "Why didn't you tell me?"

I shook my head, the tears falling freely now as I clutched at the wet fabric of my gown. "I was afraid," I whispered, my voice trembling with emotion. "I didn't know how to tell you... I didn't want to disappoint you..."

Edmund closed the distance between us in two swift steps, his arms wrapping around me in a tight, protective embrace. I collapsed against him, the sobs wracking my body as I finally let go of the last of my defenses. The fear, the guilt, the shame—I let it all out, crying into my brother's chest as he held me close.

"Hush, Isabella," he murmured, his voice thick with emotion. "It's going to be all right. We'll figure this out."

His words were a balm to my aching heart, and I clung to him, my hands gripping the fabric of his coat as if it were a lifeline. For so long, I had been carrying this burden alone, terrified of what would happen when the truth came out. But now, in Edmund's arms, I felt a glimmer of hope—a fragile, tentative hope that maybe, just maybe, I didn't have to face this alone.

As the sobs began to subside, Edmund gently pulled back, his hands resting on my shoulders as he looked down at me with a mixture of sadness and determination. "We'll get through this, Isabella," he said firmly. "But we need to act quickly. The longer we wait, the worse it will be."

I nodded, wiping at my tear-streaked face as I tried to regain some semblance of composure. "What are we going to do?" I asked, my voice small and uncertain.

Edmund's expression hardened, his jaw tightening with resolve. "First, we need to make sure you're taken care of. No more hiding, no more secrets. I'll handle the rest."

The weight of his words settled over me, and I knew that he was right. The time for hiding was over. The truth was out now, and there was no going back.

But as I looked up at my brother, his strong, reassuring presence a source of comfort in the midst of my fear, I knew that whatever came next, we would face it together. And for the first time in weeks, I allowed myself to believe that maybe—just maybe—everything would be all right.

25

The Bitter Honesty

After the tears had finally subsided and my emotions had calmed enough to think straight, Edmund gently led me upstairs to my chambers. The heaviness in the air lingered, but there was also a sense of relief—finally, the truth was out. I no longer had to bear this burden alone.

Alice, our trusted maid, had been waiting for us, her usual cheerful demeanor replaced with one of concern as she helped me out of the damp gown. The soup had soaked through the fabric, clinging to my skin and adding to the discomfort that had been mounting for weeks. With practiced efficiency, Alice brought a fresh dress, one that was looser and more comfortable, with none of the constriction of my usual attire.

"Thank you, Alice," I murmured as she fastened the last button. She gave me a small, sympathetic smile, her eyes filled with understanding. She had known, of course. She had been with me through the worst of the morning sickness and the nights when I couldn't sleep. But she had never pried, never asked questions. For that, I was grateful.

Once Alice had left the room, Edmund took a seat in the armchair by the fireplace, his expression serious as he watched me settle onto the edge of the bed. The fire crackled softly in the hearth, filling the room with warmth, but the tension between us had not fully dissipated.

We sat in silence for a few moments, the only sound the occasional pop of the firewood. I could feel Edmund's eyes on me, studying me, trying to make sense of everything that had just been revealed. Finally, he spoke, his voice soft but tinged with the weight of his concern.

"How far along are you, Isabella?"

I bit my lip, hesitating as I tried to recall the timing. Everything had become a blur over the past few months—the secret meetings, the whirlwind of emotions, the fear that had taken root in my heart. "I'm not entirely sure," I admitted, my hands clasped tightly in my lap. "I think... I might be four months along, perhaps a little more."

Edmund's brow furrowed, his gaze dropping to the slight swell of my belly, now more visible without the tight restrictions of the corset. He sighed heavily, the sound filled with frustration and resignation. "Four months... And when did you plan to tell me? After the baby was born?"

His words hit me like a slap, and I felt the sting of guilt flare up in my chest. My breath caught in my throat, and for a moment, I couldn't bring myself to meet his eyes. The reality of how long I'd been hiding this from him, how I'd allowed my fear and uncertainty to keep me silent, weighed on me like a heavy stone. My hands instinctively moved to my belly, cradling the slight curve that I had tried so hard to conceal.

"I... I don't know," I stammered, my voice breaking as the tears threatened to spill over. "I didn't think it would come to this, Edmund. I thought I could keep it hidden, just for a little while longer. I was so afraid of disappointing you, of facing what this all means..."

My voice trailed off as the tears finally escaped, rolling down my cheeks. I tried to blink them away, but they kept coming, a flood of emotion that I could no longer hold back. The room seemed to close in around me, the walls pressing in as I realized the enormity of what I had done—what I had kept from him.

"When you spread the pregnancy scandal, did you know you were pregnant? Did you do it on purpose?"

I looked away, guilt gnawing at me as I realized how much I had kept from him. "I didn't know, Edmund," I whispered. "I didn't know I was pregnant when... when I made that foolish announcement at the salon. It was all just part of a dare. A scandal to stir up the gossip and nothing more."

Edmund's eyes widened, a mix of disbelief and concern crossing his features. "A dare? Isabella, do you have any idea how reckless that was? To announce something like that in front of everyone... do you realize the gravity of what you've done? The entire city has been buzzing with rumors for weeks. And now... now it's not just a scandal. This is real. There's a child involved."

" I know I've made a mess of everything," I murmured, my throat tight. "But I didn't think it would lead to this. I thought it was just a harmless prank, something that would blow over in a few days. I didn't know... I swear I didn't know I was pregnant at the time. And I never imagined..." I trailed off, unable to finish the thought.

Edmund ran a hand through his hair, clearly struggling to keep his emotions in check. "Isabella, this is more than just a prank gone wrong. You've put yourself—and our entire family—in a precarious situation."

I nodded, tears welling up in my eyes as the reality of the situation settled over me once more. "I know, Edmund. I realize that now. But at the time... I was scared. I didn't know how to tell you, or how to face the consequences of what I'd done."

He sighed again, the frustration evident in his voice. "And what about the father? Does he even know?"

I shook my head. "He doesn't know that I'm carrying his child. I haven't told him."

"You have to be honest with me. Who is the father?"

The question I had been dreading. I had known it was coming, but hearing it spoken aloud made my heart clench with fear. I took a deep breath, steeling myself for what was to come. "It's Cassian," I said quietly, my voice barely above a whisper. "Cassian Cavendish."

Edmund's expression darkened, his jaw tightening as he absorbed this new information. "Cassian Cavendish," he repeated, his tone laced with disbelief. "The second son of the Cavendish family?"

"Yes," I confirmed, my voice wavering. "The second son."

He leaned back in his chair, his fingers drumming against the armrest as he considered this. "Cassian... He's not the heir. He has no title, no substantial inheritance. Isabella, you know what this means, don't you?"

I nodded, understanding the implications all too well. "I do. But Edmund, it wasn't supposed to be like this. We never planned for any of this to happen."

Edmund shook his head, his frustration evident. "That may be true, but it doesn't change the reality of the situation. You're carrying his child, Isabella. This isn't just about you anymore. It's about the future of our family, and the consequences of this will affect all of us."

"I'm sorry, Edmund...I'm sorry..."

Edmund rubbed his temples, his frustration clear. "Being the second son in a family like the Cavendishes... It's not the same as being the heir. Cassian has no title, no estate to inherit. He'll be expected to make his own way, and that usually means a career in the military, the church, or some business venture. But none of that compares to the life you were meant to have, Isabella. The life you deserve."

Tears welled up in my eyes again, and I struggled to keep them at bay. "I know, Edmund," I whispered, my voice thick with emotion. "I know all of that. But I care for him... I thought maybe we could—"

Edmund cut me off gently, his voice softening. "Isabella, I'm not questioning your feelings. But you need to understand the realities of this situation. Cassian is a good man, I'm sure, but he's not in a position to offer you what you've been raised to expect. This child... It complicates everything."

Tears welled up in my eyes again, and I struggled to keep them at bay. "I don't know what to do, Edmund," I confessed, my voice trembling. "I don't know how to fix this."

Edmund's expression softened, and he reached out to take my hand, squeezing it gently. "We'll figure it out, Isabella. But But you have to be honest with me, and with yourself. We need to talk to Cassian, and see where he stands in all of this. He deserves to know, and we need to find out if he's willing to take responsibility."

I nodded, feeling the weight of the decision that lay ahead of us. Edmund was right—Cassian needed to know, and we had to face this situation head-on, no matter how daunting it seemed. But as I looked into my brother's eyes, filled with concern and determination, I knew that whatever happened, I wouldn't have to face it alone.

"Cassian may not be able to offer you much in terms of wealth or status, but if he cares for you... If he's willing to stand by you and take responsibility, then we'll find a way to make it work."

I nodded, though my heart was still heavy with doubt. Cassian's return to London had reignited old feelings, but I wasn't sure where we stood now. Would he be willing to step up, to face the consequences of our actions? Or would the reality of our situation prove too much for him to bear?

As the fire crackled softly in the hearth, I felt the weight of the future pressing down on me. The path ahead was uncertain, filled with challenges I had never anticipated. But with Edmund by my side, I knew I wouldn't have to face it alone.

And yet, even as I clung to that small comfort, I couldn't help but wonder what would happen when Cassian learned the truth. Would he stand by me, or would he walk away, leaving me to navigate the storm on my own? Only time would tell, and the uncertainty of it all was almost too much to bear.

26

The Weight of Reality

In the days following Edmund's discovery, a strange sense of relief settled over me. The secret that had weighed so heavily on my shoulders was no longer mine to bear alone, and for the first time in weeks, I could breathe without the suffocating pressure of deceit. Edmund had been more understanding than I had dared to hope, his anger giving way to a fierce protectiveness that made me feel safer than I had in a long time. He had promised to help me, to find a way out of this mess, and though the road ahead was still uncertain, knowing that I wasn't alone brought me a measure of comfort.

At home, the atmosphere shifted subtly. The tension that had pervaded every corner of the house began to dissipate, replaced by a quiet acceptance. With Edmund's support, I no longer felt the need to hide behind the constricting layers of my corset. I let Alice adjust my wardrobe to accommodate my growing belly, and while the change in my silhouette was a constant reminder of what was to come, it was also a relief not to be constantly gasping for breath.

But the growing curve of my stomach, once hidden so carefully, was now impossible to ignore. As the weeks passed, it became more pronounced, a visible sign of the life growing inside me. With every glance in the mirror, I was reminded of the reality I had tried so hard to deny, and though I was more comfortable physically, the weight of my situation pressed down on me with renewed force.

One afternoon, as I sat in my chambers, the sunlight streaming through the windows in warm, golden rays, Alice entered with a tray of tea and biscuits. She set it down on the small table by the window and then, as had become her habit lately, she knelt beside me, her eyes flickering to the rounded curve of my belly.

"Milady," she said softly, her hands hovering hesitantly before gently resting on my stomach. "It's truly remarkable, isn't it? To think that there's a little life growing inside you."

I looked down at her hands, feeling the warmth of her touch through the thin fabric of my gown. The sensation was strange, both comforting and unsettling at the same time. "Yes," I murmured, placing my own hand over hers. "It's... a miracle, in a way."

Alice smiled, her eyes shining with a mixture of awe and affection. "A miracle, indeed. I've never seen anything like it up close. It's... it's beautiful."

I forced a smile, though inside, my emotions were far more conflicted. "Beautiful, yes. But also terrifying. There's so much uncertainty, so much that could go wrong..."

Her smile faltered, and she looked up at me, concern etched into her features. "You're scared, milady. I can see it."

I nodded, unable to deny the truth of her words. "I am, Alice. I'm scared of what will happen next, of what the future holds for me, for this child. Edmund has been so supportive, but even he can't change the reality of our situation. My pregnancy is growing more obvious by the day. It won't be long before it can't be hidden at all. And then what? How will society react? How will I ever face them?"

Alice's expression softened, and she squeezed my hand gently. "You're stronger than you think, milady. You've already faced so much, and you've come through it with your head held high. Whatever happens next, you'll find a way to get through it. And you're not alone—you have your brother, and you have me."

I smiled at her words, grateful for her unwavering loyalty. "Thank you, Alice. I don't know what I'd do without you."

She returned the smile, but there was a hint of sadness in her eyes as she looked down at my belly again. "But you're right, milady. You can't hide forever. The world will know soon enough. But maybe... maybe that's not such a bad thing. Maybe it's time to stop hiding."

Her words struck a chord within me, and I felt a pang of fear mixed with something else—something that felt like acceptance. "Perhaps," I whispered, my voice trembling slightly. "But I'm not sure I'm ready."

Alice didn't push the matter further, instead turning her attention back to the task at hand. She helped me prepare for the rest of the day, her movements gentle and efficient, and though we spoke little, her presence was a comforting balm to my frayed nerves.

As the day wore on, I found myself wandering through the house, my thoughts a tangled web of fears and hopes. The rooms that had once felt like a refuge now seemed to close in around me, the walls too tight, the air too thin. I couldn't escape the growing awareness that my time of hiding was coming to an end. The child inside me was growing, pushing against the boundaries of secrecy, demanding to be acknowledged.

And then there was Edmund's promise—the quiet, determined way he had spoken of finding a solution. I knew he had been in contact with the royal family, trying to navigate the delicate politics of our situation. His efforts were a testament to his love and dedication, but they also served as a constant reminder of how precarious our position truly was.

One evening, after dinner, Edmund found me in the drawing room, where I had retreated with a book in an attempt to distract myself. He sat down beside me, his expression serious but not unkind.

"Isabella," he began, his voice low and steady, "I've been speaking with the royal family about your condition."

I looked up at him, my heart pounding in my chest. "And?"

"And they've agreed to help, as much as they can," he said, his tone careful. "But there are conditions, of course. We'll have to be discreet, to manage the narrative in a way that protects both you and the family."

I nodded, feeling a mix of relief and trepidation. "What does that mean, exactly?"

"It means we'll have to be strategic," Edmund explained, his eyes searching mine. "There's talk of arranging for you to spend some time in the countryside, away from the prying eyes of society. It would give you time to carry the pregnancy to term without the constant scrutiny. And after... well, after, we'll find a way to manage things."

The idea of leaving London, of retreating to the countryside, filled me with both hope and despair. On one hand, it would offer me a reprieve from the relentless pressure I had been under, a chance to breathe and prepare for what was to come. But on the other hand, it also felt like an exile, a forced removal from the life I had known.

"I suppose it's the best option," I said quietly, my voice tinged with resignation. "But it still feels... like I'm being hidden away. Like I'm something to be ashamed of."

Edmund's expression softened, and he reached out to take my hand. "You're not something to be ashamed of, Isabella. This situation is difficult, yes, but it doesn't define you. You're strong, and you'll get through this. And when the time comes, we'll face it together."

I squeezed his hand, grateful for his reassurance, but the fear still lingered, gnawing at the edges of my resolve. The reality of what was happening—the growing life inside me, the impending birth, the inevitable confrontation with society—was becoming impossible to ignore.

As I lay in bed that night, my hand resting on the gentle curve of my belly, I couldn't help but feel the weight of the future pressing down on me. The child inside me was a part of me, a part of my life now, and soon, the world would know. There would be no more hiding, no more pretending. The time for secrets was drawing to a close.

And though I was terrified of what that meant, of the challenges and judgments that lay ahead, there was also a part of me that felt strangely at peace. Because no matter what happened, I knew that I had the support of those who loved me—Edmund, Alice, and perhaps even Cassian.

The road ahead was uncertain, fraught with difficulties I couldn't yet foresee. But as I closed my eyes and drifted off to sleep, I allowed myself to believe, just for a moment, that everything would be all right in the end.

And for now, that was enough.

27

The Grand Ball

The night of the grand ball arrived with all the pomp and circumstance one would expect from one of London's most prominent families. The invitation had been delivered weeks ago, a gilded affair with delicate calligraphy, the kind that promised an evening of elegance and excess. Under any other circumstances, it would have been the highlight of the season—a night of laughter, music, and dancing, where the city's elite gathered to flaunt their wealth and status. But for me, it felt like the final curtain call before the inevitable.

Edmund had insisted that I attend, though I knew he was torn about it. He had been adamant that I leave London soon, retreating to the countryside where I could carry out the rest of my pregnancy away from prying eyes. But before that, there was this one last social obligation—a chance, he said, to show the world that everything was as it should be, to maintain the illusion of normalcy for just a little while longer.

I had agreed, though the thought of stepping into that ballroom filled me with dread. The rumors had not died down; if anything, they had intensified, fueled by my increasingly rare appearances in society. The walls of my gown, carefully tailored to disguise the growing swell of my belly, felt more like armor than ever. But no matter how well the fabric concealed, I could not escape the truth that lurked beneath it.

As the carriage pulled up to the grand estate, the sight of the glowing windows and the strains of music drifting out into the night only deepened the sense of unease that had been gnawing at me all day. The façade of elegance and luxury, of beauty and grace, felt like a cruel joke, mocking the turmoil that simmered just beneath the surface.

I stepped out of the carriage with Edmund by my side, his presence a comforting anchor in the sea of uncertainty that awaited me. He had always been the steady one, the one who could navigate the treacherous waters of society with ease. But tonight, even he seemed tense, his gaze sweeping over the assembled guests with an air of quiet vigilance.

"Are you sure about this?" he asked quietly as we ascended the steps, his hand resting lightly on my arm. "We can leave at any time. Just say the word."

I offered him a small, reassuring smile, though my heart was pounding in my chest. "I'll be fine, Edmund. It's just one evening."

He nodded, though the concern in his eyes didn't fade. "Stay close to me. If anyone says anything—"

"I'll handle it," I finished for him, squeezing his arm gently. "You've taught me well, remember?"

The corners of his mouth lifted in a brief, fleeting smile, and I took a deep breath as we stepped into the ballroom.

The scene before us was dazzling, the room filled with a swirl of vibrant gowns, glittering jewels, and impeccably dressed gentlemen. Chandeliers cast a warm, golden glow over everything, the light catching on the ornate decorations that adorned every surface. It was the epitome of high society, a world of opulence and privilege that I had always navigated with ease.

But tonight, I felt like an imposter, a stranger in a world that no longer welcomed me.

As we made our way through the throng of guests, I did my best to keep my head high, my smile in place. I exchanged pleasantries with those who approached, keeping the conversation light and superficial, deflecting any inquiries that veered too close to dangerous territory. Edmund remained by my side, his presence a silent deterrent to any who might have been inclined to press too far.

But it wasn't long before I felt the weight of the stares, the subtle, side-

THE GRAND BALL

long glances that seemed to follow me wherever I went. The whispers, the murmurs—they were all there, just beneath the surface, like a dark undercurrent that threatened to pull me under.

And then, just when I thought I might make it through the evening unscathed, it happened.

We were near the edge of the ballroom, watching the dancers swirl across the floor, when I heard a familiar, grating voice.

"Isabella, darling!" Lady Worthington, a dowager with a penchant for gossip and a complete lack of tact, bustled over to us, her eyes alight with the thrill of being the bearer of news. "It's so good to see you out and about. And I must say, you're simply glowing!"

I forced a smile, though my heart sank at her words. "Thank you, Lady Worthington. It's kind of you to say so."

She waved a hand dismissively, her gaze sweeping over me with an appraising look that made my skin crawl. "Oh, there's no need to be modest, dear. Everyone's been talking about it, of course. You can't hide something like that forever."

A cold wave of dread washed over me, and I could feel Edmund stiffen beside me. "I'm not sure what you mean," I said carefully, doing my best to keep my voice steady.

Lady Worthington's smile widened, and she leaned in conspiratorially, lowering her voice just enough to ensure that her words would still carry to those nearby. "Oh, come now, Isabella. There's no need to be coy. You're expecting, aren't you? Why, I dare say it's the most exciting news of the season! Congratulations, my dear."

For a moment, the world seemed to tilt on its axis, the sounds of the ballroom fading into a dull roar as her words reverberated in my mind. I could feel the eyes of the guests around us, the weight of their stares, the sharp edge of their curiosity. My pulse quickened, a surge of panic rising in my chest as I struggled to maintain my composure.

Edmund was quick to step in, his voice cold and firm. "Lady Worthington, I believe you are mistaken."

But the damage had already been done. The whispers that had once been muted now grew louder, spreading through the room like wildfire. Heads turned, eyes narrowed, and I could feel the air around me grow thick with speculation.

"I-I think you're mistaken," I stammered, my voice barely audible over the cacophony of voices that seemed to fill the space between us. "I—"

But Lady Worthington, ever oblivious to the discomfort she caused, merely laughed, a sound that grated on my nerves like nails on a chalkboard. "Oh, Isabella, you don't need to pretend with me. I've been through this myself, you know. It's nothing to be ashamed of. Why, just look at you! You're positively radiant."

I felt my breath hitch in my throat, my mind racing for a way out, a way to stop the conversation from spiraling further out of control. But the more I tried to deflect, the more persistent Lady Worthington became, her words ringing louder and louder in my ears until I could hardly think.

And then, from across the room, I saw him—Cassian. His eyes met mine, and in that moment, everything seemed to fall away. The noise, the whispers, the suffocating pressure of the crowd—all of it disappeared, leaving only the two of us in that vast, glittering ballroom.

His gaze was intense, piercing, as if he could see right through me, past the carefully constructed mask I had worn for so long. There was a question in his eyes, a silent inquiry that echoed through the space between us, demanding an answer that I wasn't sure I could give.

Lady Worthington continued to prattle on, oblivious to the tension that had gripped the room. But all I could focus on was Cassian—on the way his expression shifted from curiosity to something darker, something more akin to realization.

My heart pounded in my chest, a frantic rhythm that matched the chaos of my thoughts. I couldn't stay here, couldn't face the growing scrutiny of the crowd, couldn't bear to see the disappointment in Cassian's eyes.

I had known this day would come, had known that the truth would eventually surface. But I hadn't expected it to happen like this, in such a public, humiliating way. The reality of my situation—of the life growing inside me, of the scandal that would follow—was no longer something I could keep hidden.

28

Cassian's Realization

The grand ballroom had always been a place of comfort for me, a stage where I could play my part as the charming rake, dancing through life with little care for the consequences. But tonight, as I moved through the crowd, exchanging pleasantries and half-heartedly engaging in conversation, there was a tension in the air that I couldn't quite shake. It was as if the very walls of the room were closing in, suffocating the easy confidence that had always come so naturally to me.

I had been keeping a close eye on Isabella all evening, though I tried to convince myself that it was out of mere curiosity, nothing more. But the truth was, something about her had been gnawing at me, something that I couldn't ignore. The rumors that had been circulating through the ton were persistent, growing louder with each passing day, and though I had dismissed them at first as idle gossip, the sight of Isabella tonight had stirred a deep, unsettling feeling within me.

She looked as beautiful as ever, her gown a rich shade of deep blue that brought out the color of her eyes. But there was something different about her, something I couldn't quite place. It was in the way she carried herself, the way she avoided meeting anyone's gaze for too long, as if she were afraid of what they might see.

And then there was the subtle change in her figure, the gentle curve of her waist that hadn't been there before. It was barely noticeable, but to someone who had known her as intimately as I had, it was enough to set alarm bells ringing in my mind.

I had been about to approach her, to try and draw her into conversation, when I heard Lady Worthington's voice carry across the room. The dowager had always been a thorn in society's side, with a penchant for spreading gossip and making tactless comments at the worst possible moments. Tonight was no exception.

"Isabella, darling!" Lady Worthington's voice rang out, drawing the attention of several nearby guests. "It's so good to see you out and about. And I must say, you're simply glowing!"

I froze, the words echoing in my ears as I turned to watch the exchange. Isabella, for her part, seemed to stiffen, her smile faltering as she responded with a vague, polite comment. But Lady Worthington wasn't one to be deterred by pleasantries.

"Oh, there's no need to be modest, dear. Everyone's been talking about it, of course. You can't hide something like that forever."

My heart skipped a beat, a cold knot of dread forming in the pit of my stomach. What was she talking about? The rumors had always been just that—rumors. But now, as I watched the color drain from Isabella's face, I couldn't ignore the sickening realization that was beginning to dawn on me.

"Isabella," Lady Worthington continued, her voice dropping to a conspiratorial whisper that was still loud enough for several others to hear, "you're expecting, aren't you? Why, I daresay it's the most exciting news of the season! Congratulations, my dear."

The room seemed to tilt around me, the sounds of the ballroom fading into a dull roar as Lady Worthington's words sank in. Expecting. Pregnant. The words repeated in my mind, each one a hammer blow to the fragile sense of calm I had been trying to maintain.

I had known Isabella for years, had been closer to her than anyone else. We had shared moments of passion, of vulnerability, but this... this was something I hadn't even considered. And yet, as I looked at her now, the truth was undeniable. The slight curve of her belly, the way she had been avoiding my gaze, the rumors that had seemed so ridiculous just days ago—it all fit together in a way that left me breathless with shock.

For a moment, I couldn't move, couldn't think. All I could do was stare at Isabella, the world spinning around me as the realization hit me with the force of a tidal wave.

She was pregnant.

And if the timing was what I feared, then there was no doubt in my mind who the father was.

Me.

The shock gave way to a rush of emotions—fear, guilt, confusion, and something else, something I hadn't felt in a long time. Relief. Relief that the child she carried was mine, that it hadn't been another man who had taken my place. But even that relief was tinged with guilt, because I had never intended for this to happen, had never thought that our brief affair would lead to something so life-changing.

I needed to talk to her. Now.

Ignoring the curious glances of those around me, I crossed the room in long strides, my heart pounding in my chest. Isabella was trying to make a hasty exit, her face pale and drawn as she murmured a quick excuse to Lady Worthington, but I reached her before she could escape.

"Isabella," I said, my voice low and urgent as I grabbed her arm, stopping her in her tracks. "We need to talk. Now."

She looked up at me, her eyes wide with fear, resignation, and a trace of something else—perhaps regret, or perhaps relief that the charade was about to end. She didn't protest, didn't pull away, but I could see the tension in every line of her posture, as if she were bracing herself for the worst.

Before she could respond, Edmund stepped in with impeccable timing. "Lady Worthington," he said with a charming smile, smoothly inserting himself between her and Isabella, "I must apologize, but I believe I'm needed here."

Lady Worthington blinked, taken aback by his sudden presence, and her curiosity about Isabella was momentarily deflected by Edmund's commanding attention. "Of course, Lord Fairchild," she said, her voice tinged with intrigue, "but I do hope to speak with your sister again soon."

"Certainly," Edmund replied, his tone light but firm, leaving no room for argument. "But if you'll excuse us…"

With a polite but decisive nod, Edmund turned his focus back to me and Isabella, effectively shielding her from further questioning. He leaned in close, his voice low and urgent. "Get her out of here," he murmured, his eyes flicking to mine, full of understanding. "Take her somewhere private. You both need to talk."

I nodded, grateful for his intervention, and without another word, I guided Isabella toward a side door leading out of the ballroom. We moved quickly, the prying eyes of the guests following us as we slipped out into a quieter, more secluded part of the estate.

The tension between us was almost unbearable as I led her down a dimly lit corridor, finally stopping when we reached a small, unoccupied drawing room. Once inside, I closed the door behind us, the silence in the room heavy with unspoken words.

Isabella stood in the center of the room, her back to me, her shoulders trembling ever so slightly. I could see the effort it took for her to hold herself together, to maintain even a shred of the dignity that had been so publicly threatened moments ago.

"Isabella," I said softly, stepping closer to her, "please, let's talk. Is what Lady Worthington said true? Are you… pregnant?"

She didn't answer right away, her gaze dropping to the floor as she took a deep, shuddering breath. When she finally looked up at me, her eyes were filled with tears, her expression one of quiet despair.

"Yes," she whispered, the word barely audible, but it was enough. It was all the confirmation I needed.

The air seemed to leave my lungs in a rush, my heart pounding in my ears as I struggled to process what she had just admitted. Isabella was pregnant. She was carrying my child. The thought sent a shiver down my spine, a strange blend of fear and exhilaration that left me breathless.

"How long?" I asked, my voice hoarse. "How far along are you?"

"Four months," she replied, her voice trembling. "Almost five."

Four months. I did the math in my head, the timeline fitting together with a sickening clarity. It had been four months since our last encounter, the day that had started out as a simple picnic and had ended in something much more intimate. Four months since I had last held her, kissed her, made love to her.

And now, four months later, she was standing before me, pregnant with my child.

"Why didn't you tell me?" I asked, a mix of anger and hurt creeping into my voice. "Why did you keep this from me, Isabella? I had a right to know."

She flinched at my words, her hands clasping tightly in front of her as she shook her head. "I didn't know how," she admitted, her voice cracking with emotion. "I was scared, Cassian. I didn't know what to do, how you would react. And then the rumors started, and I... I just couldn't. I thought it would be easier to keep it to myself, to try and figure it out on my own."

"Figure it out?" I repeated, my anger flaring. "Isabella, you're carrying my child. Did you really think I wouldn't want to be involved? That I wouldn't want to help?"

"I didn't want to burden you," she whispered, her tears spilling over onto her cheeks. "You've always been so free, Cassian. I didn't want to trap you, to make you feel like you had to take responsibility for something you didn't want. I can't bear the thought of you resenting me, or the child."

Her words hit me like a punch to the gut, and I felt the anger drain away, replaced by a deep, aching guilt. She had been trying to protect me, to shield me from the consequences of our actions, even as she bore the weight of it alone.

I shook my head. "I don't feel trapped, and you're not a burden. This child... our child... is not a burden. This is as much my responsibility as it is yours, and I'm ready to face it. But more than that, Isabella... I care about you. I always have," I said softly, stepping closer to her, my hands trembling as I reached out to touch her. But I'm a fool. I should have been there for you. I should have known."

She shook her head again, her tears falling freely now as she looked up at me, her expression raw with emotion. "How could you have known, Cassian? I didn't tell you. I didn't give you the chance."

"I should have been paying more attention," I insisted, my voice thick with regret. "I should have seen what was right in front of me. But I didn't, and for that, I'm sorry. I'm so, so sorry."

For a moment, we stood there in silence, the weight of our shared guilt hanging heavy in the air between us. I could see the pain in her eyes, the exhaustion that came from carrying this secret for so long. And in that moment, all I wanted to do was hold her, to take away the burden that had been crushing her for months.

"I don't know what to do, Cassian," she admitted, her voice small and fragile. "I'm so scared. I don't know how to handle this, how to face the future."

Her vulnerability tore at my heart, and I stepped closer, pulling her into my arms. She didn't resist, collapsing against me with a sob that shook her entire body. I held her tightly, my hand gently stroking her hair as I whispered words of comfort.

"We'll figure it out," I murmured, pressing a kiss to the top of her head. "We'll figure it out together, Isabella. You don't have to do this alone anymore. I'm here now, and I'm not going anywhere."

She clung to me, her tears soaking into my shirt as she cried quietly against my chest. I could feel the fear, the uncertainty that had been eating away at her, and I wished more than anything that I could take it all away, that I could make everything better.

But I knew that this was just the beginning. The road ahead would be difficult, filled with challenges and decisions that would change our lives forever. But as I held Isabella in my arms, feeling the warmth of her body pressed against mine, I knew one thing for certain:

I loved her. I had always loved her, and nothing—not even the weight of this unexpected news—could change that.

When she finally pulled back, her eyes red and swollen from crying, I cupped her face in my hands, my heart swelling with a mixture of love and determination. "We'll face this together, Isabella," I promised, my voice steady and sure. "Whatever happens, we'll face it together."

She nodded, her eyes searching mine for reassurance, and I saw the spark of hope begin to flicker in their depths. It was fragile, tentative, but it was there, and that was enough for now.

As we stood there, close enough that I could feel the warmth of her body, my gaze drifted down to the slight curve of her belly, now more apparent without the tight constraints of a corset. The reality of it—the life growing inside her—hit me with a renewed intensity. I had known, intellectually, that she was pregnant, but seeing it... it was something else entirely.

"Isabella," I began, my voice soft and tentative as I met her gaze again. "May I... may I touch your belly?"

Her eyes widened slightly in surprise, and for a moment, she seemed to hesitate. Then, slowly, she nodded, a small, shy smile playing at the corners of her lips. "Yes, Cassian," she whispered, her voice barely audible. "You can."

Gently, almost reverently, I lowered one hand from her face to her belly, my fingers trembling slightly as they made contact with the soft fabric of her dress. Beneath the layers of cloth, I could feel the subtle firmness of her abdomen, the undeniable proof of the child we had created together.

A rush of emotions surged through me—protectiveness, awe, and a deep, abiding love that I hadn't fully realized was there until this moment. I rested my hand on her belly, my thumb tracing small circles as I marveled at the life we had brought into the world, even if it had been unplanned.

"It's... it's incredible," I murmured, my voice thick with emotion. "There's really a baby in there... our baby."

Isabella let out a shaky breath, her hand coming to rest over mine on her belly. "Yes," she replied softly, her voice filled with a mix of wonder and fear. "Our baby."

"I'm going to be a father," I said quietly, almost to myself, the reality of it finally sinking in.

"Yes," Isabella whispered, her voice trembling with emotion. "And I'm going to be a mother."

We stood there for a long moment, both of us lost in the enormity of what this meant. I felt the weight of responsibility settle over me, but there was also a profound sense of connection—a bond that went beyond anything I had ever experienced before.

"Thank you," I said quietly, lifting my gaze to meet hers once more. "Thank you for letting me be a part of this, Isabella. I know this wasn't what either of us planned, but... I'm here for you. For both of you."

She smiled then, a real, genuine smile that lit up her tear-streaked face. "I'm glad, Cassian," she whispered, her voice filled with warmth. "I'm glad you're here."

I leaned down, pressing a tender kiss to her forehead before pulling her into a gentle embrace. "We'll figure this out together," I murmured against her hair. "One step at a time."

Isabella rested her head against my chest, her arms wrapping around my waist as she let out a contented sigh. "Yes," she agreed softly. "Together."

As I held her close, my hand still resting on her belly, I felt a sense of peace settle over me—a peace that had been absent for far too long. The noise of the party distant and muted, I knew that our lives had been irrevocably changed. The future was uncertain, but as long as we were together, I knew we could face whatever challenges lay ahead.

And for the first time since I had heard those fateful words, I felt a sense of peace settle over me, a calm certainty that we would be all right. That somehow, against all odds, we would find our way through this, together.

29

A Serious Proposal

The morning sun filtered through the windows of my townhouse, casting a warm glow over the room as I paced back and forth, my thoughts racing. The events of the previous night played over and over in my mind, each memory more vivid than the last. I could still feel the weight of Isabella's belly under my hand, the undeniable proof of the life we had created together. The decision I had made in that quiet corner of the garden was one that would change both our lives forever, but it was a decision I was ready to face head-on.

I had spent the rest of the night thinking, turning over every possible outcome in my mind. I knew that my proposal would come as a shock to Isabella, that she would likely be overwhelmed by the suddenness of it all. But I also knew that this was the right thing to do—not just for the sake of our child, but because I loved her. I had always loved her, and I couldn't imagine a future without her by my side.

With renewed determination, I left my townhouse and made my way to Isabella's home. The streets were bustling with the usual morning activity, but I barely noticed the noise and commotion around me. My thoughts were consumed by what I was about to do, by the words I needed to say.

When I arrived at her door, I took a deep breath, steadying myself before I knocked. A moment later, the door opened, and Alice, Isabella's maid, greeted me with a polite smile.

"Good morning, Mr. Cavendish," she said, curtsying slightly. "Miss Isabella is in the drawing room. Shall I announce you?"

"No need, Alice," I replied, returning her smile. "I'll find my way."

She nodded and stepped aside, allowing me to enter. I made my way through the familiar hallways, the anticipation building with each step. When I reached the drawing room, I paused for a moment, gathering my thoughts before pushing the door open.

Isabella was seated by the window, her back to me as she stared out at the garden. She wore a simple morning gown, the soft fabric draping gracefully over her figure. But what drew my attention most was the subtle curve of her belly, now unmistakable at four months. The gown couldn't fully conceal it, and the sight filled me with a sense of awe and protectiveness.

She turned at the sound of the door, her eyes widening slightly in surprise when she saw me standing there. "Cassian," she said softly, her voice a mixture of surprise and uncertainty. "I wasn't expecting you."

"I know," I replied, crossing the room to stand before her. "But I couldn't wait. There's something I need to talk to you about."

She nodded, gesturing for me to sit beside her on the settee. As I did, I couldn't help but notice the way her hand rested protectively over her belly, as if she were unconsciously shielding our child from the world.

"How are you feeling?" I asked, my gaze lingering on her rounded stomach. "Is everything... all right?"

She smiled faintly, her fingers gently tracing the curve of her belly. "I'm all right, I suppose. The nausea has been less frequent lately, though the cravings have been relentless."

"Cravings?" I asked, raising an eyebrow in curiosity. "What kind of cravings?"

She laughed softly, the sound tinged with a hint of self-consciousness. "The most absurd things, really. Pickles and honey, for one. And there was a night when I couldn't think of anything but roast beef, even though it was well past midnight."

I chuckled, the image of Isabella sneaking into the kitchen in the dead of night to satisfy her cravings bringing a smile to my face. But as my gaze returned to her belly, the laughter faded, replaced by a deeper sense of purpose.

Her belly at four months was a gentle, unmistakable swell, the kind that couldn't easily be hidden, even with the cleverest of gowns. The fabric of her dress clung to her curves, the soft roundness of her stomach a visible reminder of the life growing within her. It was a sight that filled me with a mixture of emotions—pride, fear, love—all mingling together in a way that left me feeling more determined than ever.

"Isabella," I began, my voice serious as I reached out to take her hand in mine. "I've been thinking a lot about what we talked about last night. About everything that's happened, and what it means for our future."

Her expression grew wary, her fingers tightening around mine. "What do you mean, Cassian?"

I took a deep breath, steeling myself for what I was about to say. "I want to marry you, Isabella."

The words hung in the air between us, heavy with meaning. Her eyes widened in shock, her lips parting as she stared at me, struggling to process what I had just said.

"Marry me?" she echoed, her voice barely above a whisper. "Cassian, I... I don't understand."

"I mean it," I said firmly, squeezing her hand. "I want to marry you. I want to be there for you, for our child. I want to turn this scandal into something positive, something beautiful. We can raise this child together, as a family."

Her breath caught in her throat, her eyes filling with a mix of emotions—fear, uncertainty, hope. "Cassian, you don't have to do this. I never wanted you to feel like you were obligated to marry me because of the baby."

"This isn't about obligation," I insisted, my voice filled with conviction. "It's about love, Isabella. I love you. I've always loved you. And I want to spend the rest of my life with you, raising our child together."

Tears welled up in her eyes, and she looked away, her free hand resting on her belly as if seeking comfort from the life growing inside her. "But what about your freedom, Cassian? What about the life you've always wanted to live? I don't want you to feel trapped."

"I'm not trapped," I replied, my voice soft but resolute. "The life I want is with you. With our child. That's the only life that matters to me now."

She turned back to me, her eyes searching mine for any hint of doubt, any sign that I wasn't being truthful. But all she found was the certainty that had settled in my heart the moment I had realized the depth of my feelings for her.

"I'm scared," she admitted, her voice trembling. "I'm scared of what this means, of how everything will change."

"I know," I said gently, lifting her hand to my lips and pressing a kiss to her knuckles. "But we'll face it together. We'll find a way to make it work. And we'll do it because we love each other, because we want to give our child the best life possible."

She hesitated, her gaze flickering to her belly once more. The gentle curve of it, the way it pressed softly against the fabric of her gown, was a visible reminder of the responsibility that lay ahead. But it was also a reminder of the love that had brought us to this moment, the love that had created the life growing within her.

"I love you too," she whispered, her voice breaking as the tears spilled over. "But..."

I could hear the hesitation in her voice, the uncertainty that lay just beneath the surface. My heart sank as I realized that my proposal had not brought her the reassurance I had hoped for. Instead, it had only deepened the conflict within her.

"But what?" I asked gently, my voice urging her to continue.

She took a deep breath, her hand absently rubbing her belly as she searched for the right words. "But I'm so afraid, Cassian. I'm afraid of losing who I am, of becoming someone else—a wife, a mother. I don't know if I'm ready for that. And I don't want you to feel like you have to give up your life, your freedom, for me. I don't want to trap you in a marriage you don't really want."

Her words cut through me like a knife, and I could see the depth of her fear, her uncertainty, in her eyes. She wasn't rejecting me—she was struggling to reconcile her love for me with her desire to maintain her independence, her identity.

"I understand," I said quietly, though my heart ached with the realization that this wasn't going to be as simple as I had hoped. "I don't want you to lose yourself, Isabella. I love you for who you are—for your strength, your independence. And I don't want to take that away from you. But I also want to be there for you, to help you raise our child. I want us to face this together, as partners."

She nodded slowly, her eyes filled with a mix of emotions that I could barely begin to understand. "I know, Cassian. I know you mean that. But... I just need some time to think. To figure out what I really want, what's best for both of us."

I nodded, though the disappointment was hard to hide. "Of course. Take all the time you need. I'll be here, waiting, whenever you're ready."

The tension between us hung heavy in the air as we sat in silence, the weight of our unspoken fears pressing down on us. I could see the conflict in her eyes, the way she was torn between her love for me and her desire to maintain her independence. And as much as I wanted to reassure her, to take away all her fears, I knew that this was something she needed to work through on her own.

Finally, she looked up at me, her eyes filled with a quiet determination. "I promise I'll give you an answer soon, Cassian. But I need to be sure. For both our sakes."

I nodded, reaching out to gently touch her belly once more, feeling the faint movement of our child beneath my hand. It was a reminder of the life we had created together, of the future that hung in the balance.

"Take all the time you need," I said softly, my voice filled with a mixture of love and understanding. "I'll be here, no matter what."

She smiled faintly, her hand resting over mine as she looked down at her belly. "Thank you, Cassian. For understanding."

With that, we sat together in silence, the weight of our unspoken fears hanging between us. And though the future was still uncertain, I knew that whatever happened, we would face it together. But for now, all I could do was wait—and hope that when the time came, she would choose a future with me.

30

The Pact

After leaving Isabella, I found myself lingering in the dimly lit hallway, the weight of our conversation pressing heavily on my shoulders. The quiet determination in her eyes, the way she touched her belly as if grounding herself in the reality of our situation, left me with a mix of hope and fear. I knew this was not an easy decision for her, and I respected her need for time, but the uncertainty gnawed at me.

As I turned the corner, I nearly collided with Edmund, who had clearly been waiting for me. His expression was a mask of restrained anger, his jaw clenched tightly as he gestured for me to follow him. Without a word, I fell into step beside him, the tension between us palpable as we made our way to a private study.

Once inside, Edmund shut the door behind us with a quiet click, the sound resonating in the stillness of the room. He stood there for a moment, his back to me, as if gathering his thoughts. I braced myself, knowing that whatever he was about to say would not be easy to hear.

When he finally turned to face me, the fury in his eyes was unmistakable. But there was something else there too—something deeper, a protective instinct that I could only begin to understand. Edmund was not just Isabella's brother; he had been her guardian, her protector, ever since their parents had died. And now, I had put her in a situation that threatened the life he had tried so hard to secure for her.

"Cavendish," he began, his voice low and controlled, though I could hear the effort it took to keep it that way, "you have no idea how much I want to lay into you right now."

I swallowed hard, nodding in acknowledgment. "I understand," I replied quietly. "If I were in your shoes, I'd feel the same way."

He nodded, his eyes narrowing as he studied me. "You've put my sister in an impossible situation, Cavendish. She's pregnant, unmarried, and facing a future that's far more uncertain than it ever should have been. And it's all because of you."

The words stung, but I knew he was right. There was no excuse for what had happened, no way to undo the reality we were now facing. "I know," I said, my voice steady despite the turmoil inside me. "And I take full responsibility for it."

"Do you?" Edmund's voice sharpened, and he took a step closer, his anger barely contained. "Do you really understand what this means for her? For our family? Isabella deserves more than this, more than you, Cavendish. She deserves the world."

I felt a pang of guilt at his words, the truth of them sinking in. Isabella did deserve the world, and I was acutely aware of my shortcomings. I was only the second son, without a title, without the kind of wealth or status that could match what the Fairchilds had. Being the second son meant that I was often seen as less important, with fewer prospects and less influence. It wasn't a role that carried much weight, especially not in the eyes of someone like Edmund, who had dedicated his life to ensuring his sister had the best of everything.

"I know I'm not the man she was meant to be with," I admitted, my voice heavy with the weight of my own insecurities. "But I love her, Edmund. And I want to do right by her and by our child."

Edmund's eyes flickered with something—perhaps recognition of my sincerity, or perhaps just a deeper understanding of the situation we were in. He sighed heavily, running a hand through his hair as he took a step back, his anger simmering down to a more manageable level.

"I believe you," he said finally, his tone softer but still firm. "But love isn't enough, Cavendish. Love won't protect her from the scandal, from the judgment of society. It won't give her the life she deserves."

I nodded, knowing that he was right. Love alone wouldn't solve the problems we were facing. We needed something more—something that could offer Isabella the security and stability she needed, especially now that she was carrying our child.

"What do you propose?" I asked, my voice steady as I met his gaze.

Edmund paused, his expression thoughtful as he considered his words. "I can help you," he said after a moment. "Financially, I mean. I have connections, resources that you don't have. If you marry Isabella, I'll ensure that you're both taken care of. I'll provide the means for you to build a life together, one that's worthy of her."

The offer was more than generous—it was everything I needed to secure a future for Isabella and our child. But accepting it meant swallowing my pride, acknowledging that I couldn't do this on my own. It meant admitting that I wasn't enough, not on my own.

But as I thought about Isabella, about the child she carried, I knew that this wasn't about me. It was about them—about giving them the life they deserved, even if it meant accepting help that I would have otherwise refused.

I took a deep breath, the decision heavy on my shoulders, but there was no hesitation in my voice when I spoke. "I'll accept your help, Edmund," I said quietly. "For Isabella's sake, and for the sake of our child, I'll do whatever it takes to make sure they're both safe and secure."

Edmund nodded, a look of relief crossing his face, though it was tempered by the gravity of the situation. "Good," he said, his voice firm. "That's the right decision. Isabella is everything to me, Cavendish. I've raised her, protected her, and I'll continue to do so, even if it means swallowing my own pride to help you. But I expect you to treat her like the only woman in this world—like she's the most precious thing you've ever had."

"She is," I replied, my voice filled with sincerity. "I promise you, Edmund, I will do everything in my power to make her happy."

Edmund's eyes softened, and he extended a hand toward me. "Then we have an understanding," he said.

I took his hand, shaking it firmly, a silent pact between us. The sacrifices I would have to make were worth it if it meant building a life with her—a life where we could raise our child together.

31

A Sister's Dilemma

As I lay on my bed that night, the room bathed in the soft glow of moonlight filtering through the curtains, my thoughts were anything but serene. The events of the day played over and over in my mind, Cassian's voice echoing with every word of his proposal. My hands rested on my belly, now fully rounded, a gentle curve that was impossible to ignore. The reality of my situation, the life growing inside me, was no longer something I could hide, even from myself.

I felt the subtle movements of the baby beneath my palms, a reminder of the choice I had to make, a choice that would shape not just my future, but the future of the child I carried. Cassian's offer had been sincere, filled with love and the promise of a shared life, but it was also overwhelming. The prospect of marriage, of becoming a wife and mother, felt like a seismic shift in the life I had always known.

I traced the outline of my belly with my fingertips, feeling the firmness of it, the way it had grown in the past months. It was still a strange sensation, this new shape of my body, a constant reminder that my life was changing in ways I had never anticipated. And now, with Cassian's proposal, those changes felt even more imminent, more real.

A soft knock on the door pulled me from my thoughts, and I quickly sat up, smoothing the covers over my lap as I called out, "Come in."

The door creaked open, and Edmund stepped inside, carrying a small tray with a teapot and a plate of biscuits. His presence was a comfort, a steadying force in the whirlwind of emotions that had consumed me all day.

"Edmund," I greeted him with a faint smile, though my heart was still heavy with the weight of my decision. "What are you doing up so late?"

He returned my smile with one of his own, though there was a hint of concern in his eyes as he approached the bed. "I couldn't sleep," he admitted, setting the tray down on the small table beside the bed. "Thought you might want a little something to eat. You've been looking a bit peaky lately."

I chuckled softly, though I couldn't help but feel a pang of guilt at his words. Edmund had always been so protective of me, especially in these past few months, and I knew he was worried. "Thank you," I said, reaching for one of the biscuits. "I suppose I could use a snack."

He watched me for a moment, his gaze flickering to my belly, which was now fully visible even beneath the loose fabric of my nightgown. Though he didn't say anything, I could see the concern in his eyes, the questions he was too polite to voice.

"Why don't you sit down?" I offered, gesturing to the chair by the window.

But Edmund shook his head, his expression softening as he approached the bed. "No, I'll sit here with you, if that's all right."

I nodded, shifting slightly to make room for him. As he settled beside me, I could feel the unspoken tension between us, the weight of everything that had happened since the news of my pregnancy had come to light.

For a few moments, we sat in silence, the only sound the soft rustle of the curtains as the night breeze drifted in through the open window. Edmund's presence was comforting, but it also made the decision before me feel even more pressing, more urgent.

"Cassian came by earlier," I said finally, my voice barely above a whisper.

Edmund's gaze shifted to me, his brow furrowing slightly. "I heard. What did he say?"

I took a deep breath, my fingers absentmindedly tracing the curve of my belly as I tried to find the right words. "He proposed. He wants to marry me, Edmund."

Edmund's eyes widened slightly in surprise, though he quickly composed himself. "He did, did he?"

I nodded, my heart pounding in my chest as I awaited his reaction. "He was serious, Edmund. He said he loves me, that he wants to raise this child together. But... I don't know. I don't know if I'm ready for that, for everything that would mean."

Edmund was silent for a moment, his gaze thoughtful as he considered my words. Then, with a soft sigh, he reached out and placed a hand on my shoulder, a gesture of brotherly comfort that I had always relied on. "Isabella," he began, his voice gentle, "I've always wanted what's best for you. You know that. And I know this is a difficult decision, perhaps the hardest one you've ever had to make. But you need to consider what's best for you and for the baby."

"I know," I whispered, my voice trembling as I fought back the tears that threatened to spill over. "But I'm scared, Edmund. I'm scared of losing who I am, of becoming someone else's wife, of being tied down to a life that I'm not sure I'm ready for."

Edmund nodded, his expression softening as he looked at me with a mixture of concern and understanding. "I can't pretend to know what you're feeling, Isabella. But I do know that you're stronger than you think. You've always been strong, even when you didn't realize it. And whatever decision you make, I'll support you."

I felt a wave of gratitude wash over me at his words, but the uncertainty in my heart remained. "What if I lose myself, Edmund? What if I become someone I don't recognize, someone who's only defined by being a wife and mother?"

He smiled faintly, his hand gently squeezing my shoulder. "You'll always be Isabella Fairchild, no matter what. Marriage, motherhood—they don't have to change who you are. They can be a part of your life, not the whole of it. And Cassian... he seems to understand that. He loves you for who you are, not for who he wants you to be."

I bit my lip, my gaze dropping to my hands, which were once again resting on my belly. The life growing inside me, the child that would soon be born, was a constant reminder of the choices I had to make, the future that was waiting for me.

"I just don't want to make the wrong choice," I murmured, my voice barely audible.

"You won't," Edmund said firmly, his voice filled with conviction. "Whatever choice you make, it will be the right one because it will be your choice. You're not alone in this, Isabella. You have me, and you have Cassian. We'll face whatever comes together."

His words were a comfort, a balm to the fears that had been gnawing at me for days. But even as I felt the weight of his support, the decision before me still loomed large, a mountain I wasn't sure I could climb.

"Do you think I should marry him?" I asked, my voice trembling with the weight of the question.

Edmund was quiet for a moment, his gaze thoughtful as he considered his response. "I think you should marry him if you love him, if you want to build a life with him. But I also think you should marry him if you believe that together, you can give this child the best possible future. Marriage is a partnership, Isabella. It's not just about love—it's about building something together, facing the challenges of life as a team. And if you believe that Cassian is the right partner for you, then I think you should consider his proposal seriously."

His words resonated with me, the truth of them sinking in. Marriage was more than just a declaration of love—it was a commitment to build a life together, to face whatever challenges came our way as a united front. And in my heart, I knew that Cassian was someone I could trust, someone who would stand by my side no matter what.

But the fear, the uncertainty, still lingered, a shadow that I couldn't shake. I wasn't just deciding for myself—I was deciding for the child I carried, for the future we would all share.

"I just need time," I said finally, my voice thick with emotion. "I need time to think, to figure out what I really want."

Edmund nodded, his expression understanding as he gave my shoulder one last reassuring squeeze. "Take all the time you need, Isabella. But know that whatever you decide, I'm here for you. We all are."

I nodded, blinking back the tears that threatened to spill over as I met his gaze. "Thank you, Edmund. I don't know what I'd do without you."

"You'll never have to find out," he replied with a smile, his eyes warm with brotherly affection. "Now, get some rest. You've had a long day."

I nodded, feeling a small measure of peace settle over me as he stood and made his way to the door. But even as the door closed softly behind him, the uncertainty remained, a constant companion to the thoughts that swirled in my mind.

As I lay back down, my hands once again resting on my belly, I knew that the decision before me was one I couldn't take lightly. Cassian's proposal was more than just an offer of marriage—it was a promise of a future, of a life together. But it was also a step into the unknown, a leap of faith that I wasn't sure I was ready to take.

The life growing inside me, the child that would soon be born, deserved the best possible future. But what did that future look like? Was it a life with Cassian as my husband, as the father of our child? Or was it something else, something that I had yet to discover?

The answers didn't come easily, and as I drifted off to sleep, my mind was still filled with questions, with fears, with hopes. The path before me was uncertain, but one thing was clear—I couldn't make this decision alone. And no matter what I chose, my life, and the life of my child, would never be the same.

32

A Heartfelt Decision

The night passed in a blur of restless thoughts and half-formed dreams. Sleep eluded me as I lay awake, my mind churning with the weight of the decision I had to make. Cassian's proposal, Edmund's advice, and the future I envisioned for myself and my child all swirled together in a confusing, emotional storm. By the time the first light of dawn filtered through my curtains, I knew I couldn't delay any longer. I had to make a choice.

As the sun's first rays crept into my room, casting a soft, golden glow across the floor, I sat up in bed, my heart pounding with a mixture of resolve and apprehension. The night had offered no clarity, only deepened the questions that swirled in my mind. But I knew that I couldn't continue to linger in uncertainty. The time had come to face my fears and make a decision that would shape the rest of my life.

I reached for the bell pull, summoning Alice. A few moments later, she entered the room, her eyes widening slightly at the sight of me already out of bed. "Miss Isabella, you're up early," she remarked, her tone gently curious.

"I couldn't sleep, Alice," I admitted, my voice trembling slightly as I spoke. "I need to meet with Mr. Cavendish this morning. We have much to discuss."

Alice's expression softened, and she nodded in understanding. "Of course, miss. I'll help you get ready."

As she moved to the wardrobe, I took a deep breath, trying to steady my nerves. "Alice, I think... I think it's time I stop hiding," I said, my hand resting protectively over the gentle curve of my belly. "I'd like to wear something that... that doesn't hide this."

Alice turned to me, her eyes widening slightly in surprise before a warm smile spread across her face. "Yes, miss. I have just the thing."

She began to sift through the gowns hanging in the wardrobe, eventually pulling out a soft, flowing dress in a delicate shade of lavender. The fabric was light and airy, perfect for the warmth of the morning, and the empire waistline would allow the dress to drape gracefully over my growing belly, accentuating rather than concealing it.

As she helped me into the dress, I felt a strange mix of vulnerability and strength. The absence of a corset, a garment that had once been a staple of my wardrobe, now felt liberating. My body had changed, was continuing to change, and I was finally ready to embrace it. The dress, free from the constraints of stiff boning and tight laces, allowed me to move and breathe with ease, the fabric gently swaying with each step.

Alice carefully adjusted the dress, smoothing the fabric over my belly with a gentle, almost reverent touch. "You look beautiful, miss," she said softly, her voice filled with genuine warmth.

I glanced at my reflection in the mirror, and for the first time in weeks, I saw a version of myself that I recognized. The rounded curve of my belly was undeniable, a clear indication of the life growing inside me, and yet, instead of fear or shame, I felt a sense of quiet pride. This was me, all of me, and I was ready to face whatever came next.

"Thank you, Alice," I murmured, turning away from the mirror. "I need to meet with Cassian this morning. Please let him know that I'll be at the rose garden."

Alice nodded, her expression gentle as she gathered the rest of my things. "Of course, miss. I'll send word to Mr. Cavendish right away."

As she left the room, I took one last deep breath, feeling the weight of the decision that lay before me. Cassian and I were not living under the same roof—he had been staying in town, close enough to be near but not intruding on my space. It had been a delicate dance, navigating our relationship while respecting the boundaries that had been necessary for my own peace of mind.

But today, those boundaries would shift. Today, I would face him with all the fears and hopes that had been swirling inside me for so long.

When I arrived at the rose garden, the morning air was crisp and cool, the scent of dew and blooming flowers filling the space around me. The garden had always been a place of solace, a retreat from the pressures of society, and today, it would serve as the backdrop for one of the most important conversations of my life.

I spotted Cassian near the rose bushes, his back to me as he gazed at the flowers. His presence was a comforting one, a steadying force in the midst of the storm of emotions I had been battling. The sight of him, strong and sure, sent a wave of conflicting emotions through me. I loved him—there was no denying that—but the life he was offering, the life I had to choose, still felt like an uncertain path.

When he heard me approach, he turned, a smile lighting up his face when he saw me. "Isabella," he greeted me, his voice warm and affectionate. "I didn't expect to see you so early."

"I couldn't sleep," I admitted, trying to steady the tremor in my voice. "There's too much on my mind."

He stepped closer, his eyes softening as they traveled over me. I could see the moment he noticed the change in my appearance—the way the dress flowed over my belly, accentuating the life growing inside me rather than hiding it. His smile widened, and he reached out to take my hand, his touch warm and reassuring.

"You look radiant," he said softly, his voice filled with a mixture of admiration and tenderness. "I'm glad you chose to wear this."

"I thought it was time," I replied, my gaze dropping to where his hand now rested on my belly. The gentle curve was a constant reminder of the choice I had to make, and I felt a surge of emotion rise within me as I considered the future we could build together.

Cassian must have sensed my inner turmoil, for he gently guided me to a nearby bench, urging me to sit beside him. The morning sun filtered through the trees, casting dappled shadows across the ground as we settled into the peaceful setting.

"I've been thinking a lot about what you said," I began, my voice trembling slightly. "About your proposal, about our future. And I realized that... I'm scared, Cassian. I'm scared of losing who I am, of becoming someone I don't recognize."

Cassian's gaze was steady, his hand still resting on my belly as he listened. "You don't have to lose yourself, Isabella. I don't want you to change who you are. I love you for the woman you are now, and I want to build a life with that woman—not some version of you that feels trapped or confined."

His words were a balm to my troubled heart, and I felt tears prick at the corners of my eyes. "But what if I'm not ready for this?" I asked, my voice barely above a whisper. "What if I can't be the wife or mother you want me to be?"

Cassian shook his head, his thumb brushing gently over the fabric that covered my belly. "There's no perfect way to be a wife or mother, Isabella. We'll figure it out together. We'll make mistakes, we'll learn, and we'll grow—just like everyone else. But we'll do it together, as a team. And I promise you, I will be by your side every step of the way."

His sincerity, the love in his eyes, and the warmth of his touch melted the last of my defenses. The tension I had been holding onto for so long began to ease, replaced by a sense of calm that I hadn't felt in months.

"I want to be with you, Cassian," I whispered, my voice thick with emotion. "I want to build a life with you and raise our child together. But I need to do it on my terms, in a way that feels right for me."

Cassian's smile was soft, his eyes filled with understanding. "Of course, Isabella. Whatever you need, we'll make it work. I want you to feel comfortable, to feel like you have the freedom to be who you are. We'll take it one step at a time, at your pace."

My heart swelled with love and relief as I looked up at him. "There are a few conditions," I said softly, my voice gaining strength as I spoke. "I want to maintain some independence. I don't want to lose the things that make me who I am—my passions, my interests. And I want us to be partners, equals in this. I don't want to be just your wife or the mother of your child—I want to be your partner in every sense of the word."

Cassian's smile grew, his eyes lighting up with affection as he leaned in closer, pressing a gentle kiss to my forehead. "I wouldn't have it any other way," he murmured, his voice warm and tender. "You're my equal in every way, Isabella. We'll build a life together, on your terms, with your passions and interests intact. And I promise to support you in everything you do."

The tears I had been holding back finally spilled over, and I let out a shaky breath, the weight of my decision lifting off my shoulders. "Thank you, Cassian," I whispered, my voice breaking with emotion. "Thank you for understanding."

He gently wiped away my tears with his thumb, his touch soft and reassuring. "I love you, Isabella," he said, his voice filled with so much sincerity that it took my breath away. "I'll love you every day of our lives, and I'll love the child we're bringing into this world. I'll do everything in my power to make sure you never regret this decision."

As I leaned into his embrace, feeling the warmth of his arms around me, I knew that I had made the right choice. Cassian's love was unwavering, his commitment to our future unshakeable. Together, we would face whatever challenges lay ahead, as partners, as equals, as a family.

And for the first time in a long time, I felt a sense of peace, knowing that I wasn't alone. Cassian and I would walk this path together, hand in hand, ready to build a life that was filled with love, hope, and the promise of a brighter future.

33

Stepping Into the Light

As the morning light continued to grow, casting its warm glow over the garden, I felt a sense of clarity and purpose settle within me. Cassian and I had made our decision, and I was ready to embrace it fully. There was no more hiding, no more cowering behind layers of fabric or fear. If I was going to live this new life, then I would do it openly and with pride.

After our heartfelt conversation in the garden, Cassian suggested we take a walk through the city. The idea initially filled me with trepidation—London's streets were filled with eyes, and I knew that whispers would follow us wherever we went. But as I looked into Cassian's eyes, filled with love and unwavering support, I felt a surge of courage. This was my life, our life, and it was time to step into it with confidence.

I nodded at his suggestion, a small but determined smile playing on my lips. "Yes," I said, my voice steady. "Let's take a walk. I'm ready to face whatever comes."

Cassian's smile was full of pride and affection as he took my hand, leading me out of the garden and toward the city streets. I could feel the warmth of his hand in mine, the silent reassurance that he was with me every step of the way. As we walked, I noticed how he kept a protective arm around me, his hand frequently moving to rest on my belly, gently rubbing it as if to show the world that this was our child, our future.

The streets of London were bustling with activity, as they always were, but today I saw the city with new eyes. The familiar sights and sounds—the clatter of horses' hooves on cobblestone, the chatter of merchants and shoppers, the distant toll of church bells—were no longer a backdrop to my anxieties. Instead, they became a reminder that life was moving forward, that I was moving forward, and I was no longer afraid.

As we strolled through the busy streets, I could feel the eyes of passersby on us, their whispers barely concealed behind gloved hands and raised fans. I caught snippets of their conversations—"Is that Lady Isabella?" "Look at her belly, she's not hiding it anymore." "Who is the father, I wonder?"—but I refused to let their words affect me. I held my head high, my hand resting on my rounded belly with a sense of pride.

Cassian, ever the supportive partner, noticed the stares but remained unfazed. In fact, he seemed to revel in the attention, his hand resting on my belly as if to silently declare to the world that he was the father of this child, that he was standing by my side through it all. His touch was gentle but firm, a constant reminder that I was not alone in this.

As we continued our walk, we rounded a corner and found ourselves face to face with Lady Evelyn, the very woman who had set this chain of events into motion with her game of Forfeits. She was surrounded by her usual entourage, a group of well-dressed ladies who clung to her every word and mimicked her every expression. The moment she saw us, her eyes widened slightly, but she quickly composed herself, her lips curling into a subtle pout of disapproval.

"Lady Isabella," she greeted me, her tone polite but dripping with condescension. "How unexpected to see you out and about. And in such... a revealing state."

I could feel the tension in the air as her eyes flicked down to my belly, clearly visible beneath the soft fabric of my dress. Her expression was a mix of judgment and curiosity, as if she were trying to piece together how I, of all people, had ended up in this situation.

But instead of shrinking under her scrutiny, I felt a spark of defiance ignite within me. This was the woman who had dared me to create a scandal, who had delighted in watching me squirm under the weight of society's expectations. And now, here she was, trying to put me back in my place with a few well-aimed barbs.

Well, I had played her game once, and it had led me here. Now it was time to turn the tables.

"Lady Evelyn," I responded, my voice calm and clear, though laced with an edge of steel. "How lovely to see you this morning. You seem surprised by my appearance. I would have thought, given your enthusiasm for games of Forfeits, that you'd be pleased to see I've embraced the consequences of our little wager so fully."

A murmur of surprise rippled through Lady Evelyn's entourage, and I could see the faintest flicker of uncertainty in her eyes. She hadn't expected me to confront her so openly, to bring up the very game she had orchestrated to humiliate me. But I wasn't done yet.

"In fact," I continued, taking a step closer to her, "I have you to thank for this opportunity. Were it not for that game, I might never have found the courage to share my news with the world in such a dramatic fashion. And I must say, the response has been overwhelming. Did you know that His Grace, the Archbishop of Canterbury, himself has sent his congratulations?"

The mention of the Archbishop of Canterbury, one of the most influential religious figures in England, caused a visible ripple of shock to pass through the assembled ladies. Lady Evelyn's eyes widened in disbelief, her carefully composed mask slipping for just a moment.

"Yes," I continued, relishing the moment. "It seems that my little announcement, as scandalous as it may have been intended, has garnered the attention and blessings of those far more important than the idle gossip of society. His Grace was most gracious, sending his best wishes for my health and the well-being of the child."

Cassian, who had been silently watching the exchange, stepped forward, his hand still resting protectively on my belly. "Lady Isabella has handled herself with grace and dignity throughout this entire ordeal," he said, his voice carrying an unmistakable note of authority. "And she has the full support of those who truly matter. It's a shame that not everyone involved can say the same."

Lady Evelyn's composure faltered, and for a moment, I saw a flash of panic in her eyes. But she quickly recovered, her lips tightening into a thin smile. "Of course, Lady Isabella," she said, her tone now strained. "It seems you've managed to turn the situation to your advantage. How... clever of you."

"It's more than just cleverness," I replied, my voice steady and confident. "It's about facing challenges head-on and transforming them into something positive. I owe that lesson to you, Lady Evelyn. Without your little game, I might never have realized just how strong I truly am."

The crowd around us had grown silent, their eyes darting between Lady Evelyn and me as they eagerly awaited her response. But for once, the formidable Lady Evelyn seemed at a loss for words. Her entourage shifted uncomfortably, clearly unsure of how to react.

"And since we're on the subject of strength and integrity," I added, my tone sharpening, "I think it's only fair to remind everyone that while some may delight in stirring the pot, it takes true character to rise above it. It's easy to spread rumors and create scandal, but it's much harder to face the consequences with grace. I hope we can all agree that such behavior is unbecoming of anyone in our circle."

Lady Evelyn's face reddened, and for a moment, I thought she might lash out. But instead, she pressed her lips together in a tight line, giving a stiff nod. "Indeed," she said through gritted teeth. "A most valuable lesson."

Her entourage, sensing the shift in power, quickly murmured their agreements, their loyalty wavering as they eyed me with a newfound respect.

As Lady Evelyn and her entourage moved away, their heads held high but their steps a little less certain, I felt a wave of triumph wash over me. For the first time in months, I had taken control of the narrative, had refused to be a passive participant in the game that others had set in motion. I had stood up for myself, for my child, and for the life I was determined to build.

Cassian turned to me, his eyes filled with pride and admiration. "You were brilliant," he said softly, his hand moving to rub my belly once more. "I've never been more proud of you."

I smiled up at him, feeling a sense of peace settle over me. The whispers and stares of the people around us no longer mattered. What mattered was the life I was creating with Cassian, the future we were building together.

"I'm done hiding," I said, my voice firm and resolute. "If this is who I am now, then I'll embrace it fully. Let the world see. Let them talk. I have nothing to be ashamed of."

Cassian's smile was warm and affectionate, and he leaned down to press a gentle kiss to my belly, his voice filled with love as he spoke to our unborn child. "We're going to show them all, little one. Your mother is the strongest, most incredible woman I know, and together, we're going to build a life that no one can tear down."

I placed my hand over his, feeling the warmth of his touch and the strength of his support. For the first time since this journey began, I felt truly free— free from fear, from shame, from the expectations of society. I was Isabella Fairchild, soon to be Isabella Cavendish, and I was ready to face whatever challenges lay ahead, with Cassian by my side and our child in my heart.

As we continued our walk through the city, the whispers followed us, but I no longer cared. Let them talk. Let them speculate. I had made my choice, and I was ready to live it fully, openly, and with pride. The game that Lady Evelyn had set in motion was over, and I had emerged stronger, more confident, and more determined than ever.

34

The Courage

After our triumphant encounter with Lady Evelyn, Cassian and I continued our walk through the bustling streets of London. The city seemed different now, less intimidating, more familiar. The whispers and stares no longer held the power they once did; instead, they served as a backdrop to the new life I was embracing.

As we turned onto a quieter street, we spotted Lady Beatrice, my dearest friend, standing outside a small tea shop. Her eyes lit up with surprise and delight when she saw us, and she quickly made her way over, her smile warm and genuine.

"Isabella! Cassian!" she exclaimed, her voice filled with excitement as she approached us. "What a lovely surprise! I didn't expect to see you both out and about this morning."

"Beatrice," I greeted her with a smile, my heart swelling with affection for my friend. "It's good to see you. We were just taking a walk through the city."

Beatrice's eyes quickly drifted downward, and her expression shifted from delight to astonishment as she took in the sight of my belly, now fully visible beneath the soft fabric of my dress. "Isabella," she breathed, her voice tinged with awe. "Your belly... it's so big! You look absolutely radiant."

I couldn't help but laugh at her reaction, the sound light and carefree. "Thank you, Beatrice. It's been quite a journey, but I'm finally ready to embrace it fully."

Beatrice reached out and gently placed her hand on my belly, her touch filled with warmth and curiosity. "I can't believe how much you've grown," she said, her voice soft with wonder. "And to think that you've been hiding this beautiful bump behind a corset all this time. You're so brave, Isabella. I can't even imagine how uncomfortable that must have been."

I glanced at Cassian, who had remained silent since Beatrice had mentioned the corset. His expression had grown somber, and I could see a flicker of guilt in his eyes. It was clear that the thought of me enduring the discomfort of a corset while carrying our child weighed heavily on him.

"It wasn't easy," I admitted, my voice gentle as I looked back at Beatrice. "But I felt like I had no choice at the time. Society's expectations, the fear of scandal… it all seemed so overwhelming. But now, I realize that I don't need to hide anymore. This is my life, my child, and I'm going to live it on my terms."

Beatrice's eyes filled with admiration, and she smiled at me, her hand still resting on my belly. "You're incredibly brave, Isabella. I'm so proud of you for standing up for yourself and for your child. You're going to be a wonderful mother."

Her words filled me with warmth, and I felt a deep sense of gratitude for her unwavering support. "Thank you, Beatrice. That means so much to me."

As we continued to chat, Beatrice's gaze shifted to Cassian, and she raised an eyebrow playfully. "So, Cassian," she said, a teasing lilt in her voice. "I suppose it's time to officially introduce you as the father of this little one?"

Cassian's somber expression lifted slightly, and he managed a small smile as he nodded. "Yes, it's true," he said, his voice steady. "I'm the father, and I'm committed to standing by Isabella and raising our child together."

Beatrice beamed at him, her eyes twinkling with approval. "Well, I must say, I'm thrilled for both of you. It's not often that such a scandalous rumor turns out to be something so beautiful."

Cassian chuckled softly, though the hint of guilt remained in his eyes. "Thank you, Beatrice. I'm just grateful that Isabella has been so strong through all of this."

Beatrice's gaze flickered back to me, and she gave my hand a gentle squeeze.

"And you, Isabella, have proven to be even stronger than I ever imagined. I don't think I could have endured what you've gone through, especially with a belly as big as yours. It's truly remarkable."

I smiled at her words, though I couldn't help but notice Cassian's expression darken once more. The mention of my corset and the discomfort I had endured seemed to weigh heavily on him, and I could see the concern etched in his features.

Sensing the shift in the conversation, I decided to change the subject to something more hopeful. "You know, Beatrice," I began, my voice light and cheerful, "I've decided that I don't need to go to the outskirts of the kingdom to hide my pregnancy or to give birth in secret. I'm staying right here in London."

Beatrice's eyes widened in surprise, and she glanced at Cassian, who had gone completely silent. "Really?" she asked, her voice filled with curiosity. "But I thought... I mean, aren't you worried about the attention, the gossip?"

I shook my head, my resolve unwavering. "Not anymore. I've realized that hiding away would only give more power to those who want to judge and gossip. I don't need to hide. This is my life, and I'm going to live it openly and proudly. Besides, I have the support of Cassian and Edmund, and that's all I need."

Beatrice smiled at me, her eyes filled with admiration. "You're absolutely right, Isabella. You have nothing to be ashamed of, and you deserve to be surrounded by those who love and support you. I think it's wonderful that you're staying in London."

Cassian, however, remained silent, his expression unreadable. The news that I wouldn't be retreating to the outskirts of the kingdom seemed to have affected him deeply, and I could see the worry in his eyes.

As Beatrice continued to chat with me, I couldn't help but feel a growing sense of unease. Cassian had been so supportive, so determined to stand by my side, but now I wondered if my decision to stay in London had made him doubt his own role in all of this. Was he worried about the attention, the potential backlash? Or was there something else that weighed on his mind?

Finally, as Beatrice excused herself to visit a nearby shop, I turned to

Cassian, my voice gentle but firm. "Cassian, is everything all right? You've been so quiet."

He looked at me, his eyes filled with a mixture of emotions—love, concern, guilt. "Isabella," he began, his voice soft, "I'm so proud of you for making this decision, for standing up for yourself. But I can't help but feel... responsible."

"Responsible?" I repeated, confused. "For what?"

"For everything," he said, his voice trembling slightly. "For the fact that you had to endure so much discomfort, for the fear and anxiety you've felt, and now... for the decision to stay in London. I know you're doing it for yourself, but I can't help but worry that it might bring more trouble, more scrutiny."

I reached out and took his hand, squeezing it gently. "Cassian, you've been nothing but supportive. You've stood by me through all of this, and I couldn't have done it without you. But this decision... it's mine. I'm not staying in London because I feel pressured or because I want to prove something to others. I'm staying because I want to. Because I want to face whatever comes my way with you by my side."

He looked down at our joined hands, his expression softening. "I just don't want you to regret anything, Isabella. I want to protect you, to make sure you and our child are safe."

"I know," I whispered, my heart swelling with love for him. "And I'm so grateful for that. But we're in this together, Cassian. We'll face whatever comes, and we'll do it as a family. I don't need to hide, and neither do you. We're stronger together."

He looked up at me, his eyes filled with a newfound determination. "You're right," he said, his voice firm. "We are stronger together. And I promise you, Isabella, I'll be by your side every step of the way."

As we continued our walk through the city, I felt a sense of peace settle over me. The future was still uncertain, but with Cassian by my side, I knew I could face whatever challenges lay ahead. Together, we would build a life filled with love, strength, and the unwavering support of those who truly mattered.

And as we walked hand in hand, I felt the weight of the world lift from my shoulders. I was no longer hiding, no longer afraid.

35

The Plan Unfolds

The moment I saw the determined light in Isabella's eyes, the way she held her head high and refused to let the whispers of London society bring her down, I knew I needed to do something more for her. The guilt I felt for the situation we found ourselves in was a constant weight on my chest. Every time I saw her rounded belly, the evidence of our child growing inside her, it was a reminder of the nights she had spent suffering, the discomfort she had endured, all because of me.

I couldn't change the past, but I could make the future something beautiful. Isabella deserved that—she deserved to know just how deeply I loved her, how committed I was to standing by her side, not out of obligation, but because my heart belonged to her entirely.

After leaving Isabella that evening, I found myself wandering through the streets of London, lost in thought. I needed to plan something special, something that would show Isabella just how much she meant to me, but I wasn't sure where to begin. The ideas swirling in my mind were vague and unformed, and I knew I needed help.

That's when it hit me—Lady Beatrice. She was not just Isabella's closest friend, but also someone who understood Isabella's heart better than anyone else. If I was going to plan something meaningful, something that would truly touch Isabella, I needed to speak with Beatrice. She would know exactly what would make Isabella's heart sing.

THE PLAN UNFOLDS

Without wasting any time, I made my way to Lady Beatrice's townhouse. When I arrived, Beatrice greeted me with a curious smile, clearly surprised by my unexpected visit.

"Lord Cavendish," she said, raising an eyebrow as she ushered me inside. "What brings you here at this hour? Shouldn't you be with Isabella?"

I offered her a small, somewhat sheepish smile. "I needed to speak with you, Lady Beatrice. It's about Isabella."

Her expression softened, and she led me to the drawing room, where we could speak privately. "Of course. What's on your mind?"

I took a deep breath, trying to find the right words. "I want to do something special for her, something that shows her how much I love her. I know she's been through so much because of me, and I want to give her something meaningful. But... I'm not sure where to start."

Beatrice's eyes sparkled with interest, and she leaned forward slightly. "Cassian, that's a wonderful idea. Isabella has been incredibly strong, but I know she would appreciate a gesture that shows just how much you care. Do you have any ideas so far?"

"Well," I began, hesitating slightly. "I was thinking about recreating a special memory, something that reminds us both of why we fell in love in the first place. But I don't know if that's enough. I want it to be something that truly touches her heart, something that she'll remember forever."

Beatrice smiled, her expression warm and thoughtful. "You're on the right track, Cassian. Isabella isn't someone who is easily swayed by grand gestures for the sake of them. It needs to be personal, something that resonates with her. Do you remember how the two of you first met?"

I nodded, a small smile tugging at the corners of my lips as I recalled that day. "Of course. It was at a charity ball. We were introduced by mutual acquaintances, but what I remember most was how we ended up sneaking away from the crowd to talk in the gardens. She was so different from anyone I'd ever met—witty, independent, not afraid to speak her mind."

Beatrice's smile widened. "Exactly. Why not recreate that moment? But this time, make it even more intimate. Remind her of why she fell in love with you, and why you fell in love with her. It doesn't have to be extravagant—it just needs to be meaningful."

The idea began to take shape in my mind, and I felt a surge of excitement. "I could arrange for a private dinner in a garden, with all her favorite foods, and maybe even some of those flowers she loves so much... lavender and roses. And I could... I could write her a letter, like the ones we exchanged when we were first getting to know each other."

Beatrice's eyes softened, and she nodded approvingly. "Yes, that's perfect. Isabella has always cherished those letters. And if I may suggest, perhaps you could include something that acknowledges the new life you're about to share. A symbol of your future together. It doesn't have to be anything too grand—just something that shows her you're thinking about the life you'll build as a family."

I thought about it for a moment, then a new idea blossomed in my mind. "A locket," I said, the idea coming to life. "I could give her a locket with a space for a picture of our child when they're born. It's something she can keep close to her heart, a reminder that we're in this together."

Beatrice's eyes shone with approval, and she reached out to place a hand on mine. "That's beautiful. Isabella will be deeply touched by such a thoughtful gesture."

With Beatrice's guidance, the plan began to take shape more clearly in my mind. We spent the next hour refining the details, discussing how to create the perfect setting for the evening. Beatrice's insight was invaluable—she knew exactly what would make Isabella feel cherished and loved.

By the time I left Beatrice's townhouse, I felt a renewed sense of purpose. The guilt that had been weighing on me was still there, but now it was accompanied by a determination to make things right. I wanted to create a moment that would remind Isabella of how much she was loved, how deeply I cared for her, and how committed I was to building a future together.

As I walked through the quiet streets of London, my mind was filled with thoughts of the plans I would put into action. With Beatrice's help, I was ready to show Isabella just how much she meant to me, and how excited I was for the life we were about to share.

36

A Night to Remember

The night had finally arrived. The city of London, usually so bustling and noisy, seemed to hold its breath as I prepared for the evening that would determine so much about my future with Isabella. The air was cool, tinged with the sweet scent of blooming flowers and the faint hint of the river's breeze. I could feel the weight of the night pressing on my chest, my heart pounding in sync with the distant echoes of horse hooves on cobblestone streets.

Everything had to be perfect. Every detail, every candle, every flower had been chosen with care, each one a reflection of the love I held for Isabella. This wasn't just about showing her how much I loved her—it was about proving to myself and to society that our love was real, untainted by scandal or gossip. Tonight was our chance to redefine our story.

The setting I had chosen was nothing short of magical. Nestled within the heart of London was a secluded garden, a hidden paradise that few knew about. High stone walls, covered in a tapestry of ivy and delicate climbing roses, enclosed the space, creating an intimate sanctuary away from prying eyes. I had discovered this garden during one of my many walks through the city, and from the moment I laid eyes on it, I knew it was the perfect place for tonight.

As I walked through the garden, overseeing the final preparations, I couldn't help but feel a swell of pride. The lanterns, carefully hung from the branches of ancient oak trees, cast a warm, golden glow that bathed the garden in a soft, ethereal light. The pathways were lined with candles, their flames flickering gently in the breeze, leading the way to the center of the garden where a small fountain bubbled quietly, its waters catching the light in a mesmerizing dance.

The table for two had been set beside the fountain, draped in fine linens and adorned with fresh flowers—lavender and roses, the very flowers Isabella loved. I had spared no expense, ensuring that everything from the silverware to the crystal glasses was of the finest quality. But it wasn't the luxury that mattered; it was the thought, the care that had gone into every decision, every detail.

On the table, placed with deliberate care, was the locket I had chosen for Isabella. It was a delicate piece, engraved with intricate patterns of vines and flowers, designed to hold a picture of our child when they were born. I imagined Isabella wearing it close to her heart, a symbol of our future, of the life we were about to create together.

The night was cool, but I hardly noticed. I was too caught up in the moment, in the anticipation of what was to come. The guests would be arriving soon, a carefully selected group of people whose opinions held weight in society. These were the very same people who had whispered behind their fans about Isabella's supposed scandal, who had judged her without knowing the truth. Tonight, they would see the real story, the love that had brought us to this moment.

As the first guests began to arrive, I greeted them with a calm demeanor, though inside, a storm of nerves raged. Every new arrival brought a fresh wave of anxiety—what would they think? Would they see this for what it was, a genuine expression of love, or would they dismiss it as yet another attempt to smooth over a scandal?

But I kept my composure, reminding myself of the purpose of this night. It wasn't about winning approval, though that would be a welcome outcome. It was about Isabella, about showing her just how much she meant to me, and about making a public declaration that would leave no room for doubt.

And then, the moment I had been waiting for arrived. Isabella entered the garden, escorted by Lady Beatrice, who had been an invaluable ally in planning this evening. The sight of her took my breath away. She looked radiant, her beauty heightened by the soft glow of the lanterns. She wore a gown of soft blue, the fabric flowing gracefully around her, accentuating the gentle curve of her belly—now proudly visible for all to see.

For a moment, I couldn't move. I was transfixed by the sight of her, by the quiet strength she exuded as she walked into the garden. Our eyes met across the distance, and in that instant, I knew that everything I had done, every detail I had agonized over, had been worth it. This was the woman I loved, the mother of my child, and tonight, I was going to show her—and the world—just how much she meant to me.

The evening unfolded in a way that felt almost dreamlike, every moment carefully orchestrated to create an atmosphere of romance and intimacy. The guests mingled, their conversations quiet and respectful as they admired the beauty of the garden. But beneath their polite smiles, I could sense their curiosity, their need to understand the true reason behind this event. I knew they were waiting for the moment when I would reveal the purpose of the evening, and I could feel the anticipation building.

As the sun dipped below the horizon, the sky painted in hues of pink and orange, I knew it was time. The lanterns flickered to life, casting a warm, golden glow over the garden, creating a scene that felt almost magical. The soft strains of a waltz drifted through the air, the very same piece that had played the night Isabella and I first met.

I stepped forward, taking my place at the center of the gathering. The murmur of conversation faded away, replaced by a hush of anticipation as all eyes turned to me. The weight of the moment pressed down on me, but I welcomed it. This was what I had been building toward, the culmination of all my plans and hopes.

"Ladies and gentlemen," I began, my voice carrying over the quiet garden. "Thank you all for joining us this evening. I know many of you have heard the rumors, the stories that have circulated about Lady Isabella and myself. Tonight, I want to set the record straight."

I paused, letting the weight of my words sink in. I could feel the tension in the air, the curiosity in the eyes of the guests as they waited for me to continue. "What began as a rumor, a scandalous whisper in the halls of London society, has brought us to this beautiful night. But what you may not know is that this is not a story of scandal, but a story of love."

My eyes found Isabella's, and I felt a rush of emotion as I saw the love and trust reflected in her gaze. "From the moment I met Isabella, I knew she was different. She was strong, independent, unafraid to speak her mind. She challenged me, made me think, and made me see the world in a new way. And as we grew closer, I realized that what I felt for her was something rare and beautiful. It was love."

The guests remained silent, their attention fully on me as I spoke. "But as you all know, life is not without its challenges. Isabella and I found ourselves in a situation that many would consider difficult, even scandalous. But instead of running from it, instead of hiding or denying what was happening, Isabella faced it with a strength and grace that I have come to admire more than words can express."

I felt my voice tremble slightly as I spoke the next words, but I forced myself to continue, to lay bare the truth for everyone to see. "Isabella is carrying my child, our child, and I could not be more proud of her, or more excited for the life we are about to build together. I love her, and I want the world to know it."

I could see the shift in the faces of the guests, the skepticism giving way to something warmer, more understanding. They were beginning to see what I had known all along—that this was no scandal, but a story of love and commitment.

With deliberate steps, I moved toward Isabella, each one feeling like a heartbeat, steady and sure. When I reached her, I took her hand in mine, holding it tightly as I looked into her eyes. "Isabella," I said, my voice low and filled with emotion, "I love you more than I can ever express. I want to spend the rest of my life with you, raising our child, building a future together. Will you marry me?"

The world seemed to hold its breath as I waited for her response. Time stretched, the silence around us thick with tension. I could see the tears welling up in her eyes, the emotions she was struggling to keep in check. For a moment, I feared that I had overwhelmed her, that my grand gesture had been too much.

But then, slowly, Isabella nodded, a radiant smile breaking across her face. "Yes, Cassian," she whispered, her voice trembling with emotion. "Yes, I will marry you."

Relief flooded through me, so powerful that it nearly brought me to my knees. I pulled her into my arms, holding her tightly as the applause erupted around us. The guests, who had come expecting to witness a scandal, were now on their feet, clapping and cheering, offering their congratulations and well-wishes.

As I held Isabella close, the tension of the past few months seemed to melt away. We had faced so much together, but now, standing in this beautiful garden, surrounded by the support of our friends and family, I knew that we could face anything the future held.

When the applause finally subsided, I gently pulled back, looking down at Isabella with all the love I felt for her shining in my eyes. "You've made me the happiest man in the world," I whispered, pressing a soft kiss to her forehead.

She smiled up at me, her eyes filled with love and hope. "And you've given me everything I could ever want," she replied, her voice soft but filled with conviction. "I love you, Cassian. I always have, and I always will."

As we stood there, surrounded by the beauty of the garden and the warmth of the people who cared about us, I knew that this was the beginning of a new chapter in our lives. A chapter filled with love, with joy, and with the promise of a bright future.

And as I looked around at the smiling faces of our guests, I knew that we had done it. We had turned a scandal into something beautiful, something that everyone could celebrate. Our love had triumphed, and the future was ours for the taking.

37

A Joyous Celebration

The day had finally arrived. I stood in my dressing room, gazing at my reflection in the large mirror before me. The sunlight streamed through the windows, casting a warm, golden glow that seemed to reflect the joy and anticipation that filled the air. My wedding dress, a stunning creation of ivory silk and lace, hugged my body in all the right places, accentuating the curve of my now six-months-pregnant belly. The gown had been tailored to fit my changing shape perfectly, and I was proud to wear it.

This was no ordinary wedding. As I looked at my reflection, I couldn't help but marvel at the journey that had brought me to this moment. The rumors, the scandal, the uncertainty—none of it mattered anymore. Today, I was marrying the man I loved, the father of my child, and I was doing it with my head held high and my heart full of joy.

Alice, my ever-faithful maid, bustled around me, making the final adjustments to my dress. "You look absolutely radiant, my lady," she said, her voice filled with genuine admiration.

I smiled at her, my heart swelling with gratitude. "Thank you, Alice. I couldn't have done any of this without you."

She blushed slightly, clearly pleased by the compliment. "It has been an honor to serve you, Lady Isabella. And today... well, today is the culmination of everything you've worked so hard for. You've shown London what true strength and courage look like."

I nodded, my smile widening as I placed a hand on my rounded belly. "It feels surreal, doesn't it? To think that a few months ago, I was hiding away, terrified of what society would think. And now... now I'm about to marry the man I love, with all of London watching."

Alice laughed softly, smoothing out a final wrinkle in my gown. "And they'll be watching, indeed. But I have no doubt that they'll be watching with admiration and respect. You've started something, my lady. Who knows how many other women will find the courage to live their truth because of you?"

Her words gave me pause. I hadn't considered that my decision to embrace my pregnancy and marry Cassian openly could have a wider impact. But as I thought about it, I realized she was right. In a society that valued appearances and propriety above all else, my choice to proudly show off my growing belly on my wedding day was a quiet revolution of sorts. It was a statement that women didn't need to hide, to shrink themselves to fit society's expectations. They could embrace who they were, flaws and all, and still find happiness.

With one final glance in the mirror, I took a deep breath, steeling myself for the day ahead. "It's time," I said softly, turning to face Alice.

She nodded, her eyes shining with tears of joy. "Yes, my lady. It's time."

As we made our way to the grand hall where the ceremony was to be held, I could hear the murmur of voices growing louder. All of London society had been invited to witness this day—the same people who had once whispered about my supposed scandal were now here to celebrate my marriage. The irony wasn't lost on me, but I felt no bitterness, only a sense of peace and contentment.

When I reached the entrance to the hall, my brother Edmund was waiting for me. Dressed in his finest attire, he looked every bit the proud older brother. His eyes softened as he saw me, and he offered me his arm with a smile. "You look beautiful, Isabella," he said, his voice thick with emotion.

"Thank you, Edmund," I replied, my voice equally emotional. "And thank you for standing by me through everything."

He patted my hand gently. "There was never any question of that. You're my sister, and I'll always be here for you. Now, let's go make you a married woman."

With a deep breath, I took his arm, and together we stepped into the hall. The room was filled with people—men and women dressed in their finest clothes, their eyes all turning toward me as I entered. But instead of the judgment or whispers I might have once feared, I saw only smiles, admiration, and respect. The air was filled with the scent of flowers—roses, lavender, and lilies—creating a heady fragrance that matched the beauty of the scene before me.

At the end of the aisle stood Cassian, waiting for me with a look of pure love and devotion in his eyes. He was dressed impeccably, his usual rakish charm softened by the depth of emotion that was evident on his face. As our eyes met, I felt my heart swell with love for him. This was the man I was going to spend the rest of my life with, the father of my child, my partner in all things.

As Edmund and I walked down the aisle, I could feel the weight of the moment settling over me. Each step brought me closer to the future I had once been so unsure of, but now embraced fully. I held my head high, my hand resting gently on my belly, and I could feel the strength and courage that had brought me to this point.

When we reached Cassian, Edmund gently placed my hand in his. The warmth of Cassian's touch sent a wave of comfort through me, grounding me in the present. The ceremony began, the officiant's voice a steady, calming presence as he led us through the vows that would bind us together.

As we exchanged vows, I felt the words resonate deep within me. Every promise, every declaration of love, felt like a reaffirmation of everything we had been through together. Cassian's voice was strong and clear, his eyes never leaving mine as he spoke his vows. When it was my turn, I felt a surge of emotion so powerful it nearly took my breath away. But I spoke my vows with confidence, my voice unwavering as I promised to love, honor, and cherish him for the rest of our lives.

Finally, the moment came. "I now pronounce you husband and wife," the officiant declared, his voice filled with warmth. "You may kiss the bride."

Cassian smiled at me, a look of pure joy on his face as he leaned in and pressed his lips to mine. The room erupted in applause, the sound echoing off the walls as our guests celebrated our union. But in that moment, all I could focus on was Cassian—the feel of his lips against mine, the warmth of his arms around me, the love that radiated from him.

As we pulled apart, I glanced around the room, taking in the smiles, the cheers, the expressions of joy on the faces of our friends and family. This was no longer a room filled with whispers and judgment. It was a room filled with love, support, and celebration.

The reception that followed was a blur of laughter, music, and dancing. The joy that filled the air was infectious, and I found myself caught up in the happiness of the day. Everywhere I looked, people were smiling, congratulating us, sharing in our happiness. Cassian was never far from my side, his hand often resting on my belly, a silent gesture of love and protection.

As the night wore on, I took a moment to step outside, needing a brief respite from the excitement. The garden was quiet, the lanterns casting a soft glow over the flowers and trees. I placed a hand on my belly, feeling the gentle movements of our child within me. A smile spread across my face as I thought about the future—the life that Cassian and I were going to build together.

I heard footsteps behind me, and I turned to see Cassian approaching, a soft smile on his face. "I thought I'd find you out here," he said, his voice gentle as he joined me.

"I just needed a moment," I replied, leaning into him as he wrapped an arm around my shoulders. "It's been such a whirlwind, and I wanted to take it all in."

Cassian placed a hand over mine on my belly, his touch warm and reassuring. "It's been quite the journey, hasn't it?" he said softly. "But I wouldn't trade it for anything. I'm so proud of you, Isabella. You've faced everything with such strength and grace. I'm the luckiest man in the world to have you as my wife."

I looked up at him, my heart overflowing with love. "And I'm the luckiest woman to have you by my side, Cassian. I never imagined this is where our journey would take us, but I'm so grateful it did."

We stood there in the quiet of the garden, the night air cool and refreshing, the sounds of the celebration faint in the distance. It was a moment of peace, of reflection, and of deep contentment. I knew that life would bring its challenges, but with Cassian by my side, I was ready to face them all.

As we turned to head back inside, I paused for a moment, looking out over the garden. "You know," I said thoughtfully, "I think this is just the beginning. We've faced so much already, and yet... I feel like the best is still to come."

Cassian smiled, his eyes filled with love as he looked at me. "I think you're right, Isabella. The best is yet to come, and we'll face it together. As a family."

Hand in hand, we returned to the celebration, ready to embrace the future with open hearts and minds. The love that had brought us together, that had weathered every storm, would guide us through whatever came next. And as we stepped back into the warmth and joy of our wedding day, I knew that our story was far from over.

It was just beginning.

38

Love Making

The door clicked shut behind us, sealing us within the sanctum of our marital bedroom. We were now on our first night as a married couple, and the anticipation was palpable. Cassian's arms encircled me from behind, his lips finding the nape of my neck with a hunger that spoke of both reverence and desire. His hand caressed the swell of my belly, the life within eliciting a gentle kick as if in greeting to its father. The warmth of his touch through the fabric of my nightgown was a balm to the fluttering nerves dancing in my stomach.

"Hello, little one," Cassian murmured against my skin, his voice a melodic whisper that reverberated through me. "Your mama and I have been waiting for this night."

Cassian wrapped his arms around me and kissed me deeply. His hands instinctively found their way to my belly, where our child was growing. We stood there, locked in a passionate embrace, as we continued to kiss. My hands began to wander, and I started to unbutton Cassian's shirt. He responded in kind, slipping his hand underneath my nightgown.

With a groan, Cassian lifted me up and pressed my back against the wall. I wrapped my arms around his neck, while my legs were wrapped around his waist. The position was dangerous, but I trusted him completely. My belly was pressed against his, and I could feel his hardened length playing against my clitoris. He kissed my neck and nibbled my earlobes, before moving down to my breasts. He sucked and pinched my nipples, causing me to moan with pleasure. As he continued to explore my body, I could feel myself becoming wet with desire. I reached down and began to touch him, feeling his hard cock through his pants. He groaned with pleasure as I rubbed him, his hips thrusting against my hand.

He began to enter me, slowly at first, and then with sharp, repeated thrusts. I sighed with pleasure as he filled me up. I wrapped my legs around him, pulling him deeper inside of me. We moved together in a rhythm that was both primal and beautiful, our bodies becoming one.

However, I soon began to feel uncomfortable with this position. My belly tightened and I could hardly breathe. Cassian must have sensed my discomfort, as he gently set me down on the table, his eyes filled with a desire that sent shivers down my spine. I wrapped my legs around him, pulling him closer to me. He spread my legs apart and entered me again, this time with more control. He thrust in and out of me, each movement sending waves of pleasure through my body. Our bodies moved together in a rhythm that was both primal and beautiful.

"Yes, Cassian," I moaned, as he thrust into me. "Harder, harder."

Cassian responded by picking up the pace, his hips moving faster and faster. I could feel myself getting closer and closer to the edge.

"Don't stop," I begged, as I felt the familiar stirrings of an orgasm building inside me.

Cassian didn't disappoint. He continued to thrust into me, his fingers finding their way to my clit. I cried out while holding my pregnant belly as I came, my orgasm ripping through me like a tidal wave. Cassian followed soon after, his own release triggered by mine.

We lay there for a moment, our bodies spent and our breaths heavy. Cassian leaned down and kissed me softly, his lips warm against mine.

"I love you," he whispered.

"I love you too," I replied, smiling up at him.

Cassian and I had just finished a passionate lovemaking session. Our bodies were slick with sweat, and our breathing was heavy. Cassian looked down at me with a satisfied smile and said, "Let me help you clean up, love."

He picked me up gently and carried me to the bathroom. Cassian helped me sit on the bathtub. I sank into the flowery water with a sigh of contentment. Cassian climbed in behind me and pulled me close, his strong arms wrapped around my belly.

"You feel amazing," he murmured in my ear.

I leaned back against him, feeling his hard length pressing against my bottom. "I wish we could do it again," I whispered.

Cassian chuckled. "Soon, love. But for now, let's just enjoy each other's company."

He began to wash my body, his hands gentle as they moved over my skin. I closed my eyes and let out a moan as he cupped my breasts, his thumbs brushing over my nipples.

"You like that?" he asked, his voice husky with desire.

"Yes," I breathed.

Cassian continued to touch me, his hands moving lower until they were between my legs. He began to rub my clit in slow circles, and I gasped as pleasure washed over me.

"You're so wet," he said, his voice low.

"I want you inside me," I moaned. "Do you want to do it?"

"What about our baby?"

I rubbed my wet stomach. "If we take it slow, maybe the baby will be okay."

Cassian positioned himself behind me and entered me slowly, his hands on my hips to steady me. I cried out as he filled me, my body stretching to accommodate him.

Cassian began to thrust, his pace steady and sure. I pushed back against him, meeting him stroke for stroke. The water sloshed around us as we moved together, our bodies slick with sweat and water. His thrusts becoming harder and faster as he took me from behind. I could feel myself getting close to the edge, my body trembling with pleasure.

"Yes, Cassian," I moaned. "Harder."

Cassian obliged, his thrusts becoming harder and faster. I could feel myself getting close to the edge, my orgasm building deep within me.

"Come for me, love," Cassian growled in my ear.

With one final thrust, I shattered, my orgasm crashing over me like a wave. Cassian followed soon after, his release filling me up.

We collapsed in the tub, our bodies spent and sated. Cassian pulled me close, his arms wrapped around me.

39

The Sweet and Unexpected

The wedding had been a dream—one of those rare, perfect days that left me feeling as if the world was filled with nothing but joy and possibilities. Our first night as a couple was also beautiful and unimaginable. But as Isabella and I settled into married life, reality quickly made itself known. Despite the bliss of our new union, there were challenges that came with Isabella's pregnancy, ones that neither of us could have anticipated.

It started with the morning sickness. I had thought that it would ease after the first few months, but here we were, six months into the pregnancy, and Isabella was still suffering from bouts of nausea that left her pale and exhausted. Every morning, I would wake to the sound of her retching, and my heart would ache knowing there was little I could do to help her.

One particularly rough morning, I found myself hovering in the doorway of our bedroom, watching as Isabella sat on the edge of the bed, her face drawn with fatigue. She was trying to sip some ginger tea—one of the remedies we had tried to ease her nausea—but I could tell from the look on her face that it wasn't helping much.

"Is there anything I can do, my love?" I asked, stepping forward and kneeling beside her. My hand instinctively went to her belly, rubbing gentle circles in an attempt to offer some comfort.

She gave me a wan smile, her eyes filled with affection despite her discomfort. "You're already doing more than enough, Cassian. It's just... I thought this would have passed by now."

"So did I," I admitted, feeling a twinge of frustration at my own helplessness. "If only there were something more I could do. I hate seeing you like this."

Isabella placed her hand over mine, squeezing it gently. "You're here, and that's more than enough. Besides, it's not all bad. Our little one is quite active, isn't he? Or she?"

As if on cue, Isabella's face suddenly paled again, and she quickly set the teacup aside before rushing to the basin nearby. I followed immediately, worry tightening in my chest as I watched her retch, her body trembling with the effort.

When it was over, Isabella remained bent over the basin, her breathing shallow and labored. Without thinking, I moved behind her, gently lifting her limp body into my arms and carrying her back to the bed. She didn't protest, too weak to argue as I sat down and settled her on my lap.

"There now," I whispered, wrapping my arms around her and pulling her close. I rested my hand on her swollen belly, feeling the subtle movements of our child within. "Just rest, my love. In a few weeks, all of this will be behind us, and we'll have our little one in our arms."

Isabella leaned her head against my chest, her body relaxing into my embrace as I continued to rub her belly in slow, soothing circles. "I can't wait to meet them," she murmured, her voice soft and tired. "But this part... it's harder than I expected."

"I know," I replied, pressing a gentle kiss to the top of her head. "But you're so strong, Isabella. You've been handling this with such grace, even when it's been difficult. And I'll be here, every step of the way, to make sure you and our baby are safe and comfortable."

She smiled faintly, her hand coming to rest over mine on her belly. "I'm lucky to have you, Cassian."

"No," I whispered, my voice filled with emotion. "I'm the lucky one. To have you, to have this family we're building together... it's more than I ever dreamed of."

For a few moments, we sat in peaceful silence, the gentle rise and fall of her breathing the only sound in the room. I could feel the warmth of her body against mine, the reassuring beat of her heart beneath my hand. It was a moment of quiet intimacy, a reminder of the deep bond we shared.

But then, just as I began to think she might finally be feeling a bit better, Isabella tensed in my arms, her breath hitching as another wave of nausea overtook her. I could feel her stomach clench under my hand, and I quickly helped her off my lap, guiding her back to the basin just in time.

I stayed by her side, holding her hair back and murmuring words of comfort as she endured another round of sickness. It pained me to see her like this, to feel so powerless in the face of her discomfort. But I knew that all I could do was be there for her, to offer my love and support as she navigated the challenges of pregnancy.

When the nausea finally subsided, Isabella slumped back against me, utterly exhausted. I lifted her back into my arms, holding her close as I gently rocked her, hoping to ease some of the strain she was feeling.

"You're doing so well, Isabella," I murmured, brushing a strand of hair away from her damp forehead. "Our baby is going to be so lucky to have you as their mother."

She looked up at me, her eyes glassy with fatigue but filled with love. "And you as their father," she whispered.

I smiled, leaning down to press a tender kiss to her lips. "We're in this together," I said softly. "You, me, and our little one. And soon, we'll all be together as a family."

Isabella sighed contentedly, her head resting against my shoulder as she closed her eyes. I continued to hold her, my hand resting protectively on her belly, feeling the life we had created together move within her.

* * *

Over the past few weeks, we had both marveled at the growing life inside her, the kicks and movements that had become stronger and more frequent. Every time I felt those little nudges against my hand, it was like a reminder of the incredible journey we were on together.

Still, the nights were another matter. Isabella's growing belly made it increasingly difficult for her to find a comfortable position to sleep in, which meant that sleep was often elusive for both of us. I would lie awake beside her, listening to her toss and turn, the frustration in her sighs growing with each passing minute.

One night, after hours of restless shifting, she finally gave up and sat up in bed with a huff. "I can't do this, Cassian. I feel like a beached whale."

I stifled a laugh, knowing better than to let her see my amusement. "You're not a beached whale, Isabella. You're carrying our child. You're beautiful."

She shot me a look, one that was half-annoyed, half-endearing. "Flattery will get you nowhere when I'm this uncomfortable."

I scooted closer to her, wrapping my arms around her from behind and resting my hands on her belly. "Then let me at least try to help. What if we went for a walk? Maybe the fresh air would help you relax."

She hesitated, then nodded. "All right, but only because I'm desperate for some relief."

We ended up walking through the quiet halls of our home, the moonlight streaming through the windows casting a soft glow on the polished floors. It was peaceful, almost serene, and I could feel some of the tension leaving Isabella's body as we moved. We talked quietly, our voices barely more than whispers as we discussed our hopes and fears for the baby, our plans for the future, and the little things that made us laugh.

At one point, as we stopped by a window to admire the night sky, I leaned in to kiss her. It was meant to be a gentle, reassuring gesture, but as our lips met, Isabella suddenly gasped and pulled away.

"What is it?" I asked, alarmed.

She placed a hand on her belly, her eyes wide with surprise. "I... I think I just had a contraction."

A wave of panic surged through me. "A contraction? Now? But it's too early, isn't it?"

Isabella nodded, looking just as bewildered as I felt. "Yes, it's too early. But

I definitely felt something."

For a moment, we both stood there, frozen, trying to process what was happening. Then, as if on cue, another contraction hit, and I could see the discomfort on her face.

"Cassian," she said, her voice tinged with both fear and awe, "I think we need to call the midwife."

I didn't need to be told twice. Within moments, the household was awake, and we were preparing for the possibility that our child might be arriving sooner than expected. The midwife arrived quickly, her calm demeanor doing wonders to steady my nerves, even as I hovered anxiously by Isabella's side.

"It's all right," the midwife said, examining Isabella with practiced efficiency. "This can happen sometimes—a little early activity. But it doesn't necessarily mean the baby is coming right now. Let's just keep an eye on things."

For the next few hours, we did exactly that. Isabella lay in bed, her hand gripping mine as we waited, each moment feeling like an eternity. But gradually, the contractions eased, and the tension in the room began to dissipate.

The midwife finally smiled, giving us both a reassuring nod. "It looks like it was just a bit of early excitement. The baby's still safely tucked away for now."

Isabella let out a relieved breath, her hand squeezing mine tightly. "Thank goodness."

I leaned down to kiss her forehead, my heart swelling with love and relief. "You gave me quite a scare, my love."

She smiled up at me, her eyes sparkling with a mixture of exhaustion and mischief. "I gave myself a scare, too. But I suppose it's just another reminder that our little one is going to keep us on our toes."

As the midwife left and the household began to settle down once more, I helped Isabella get comfortable in bed. This time, I pulled a few extra pillows around her, creating a cocoon of sorts to help support her growing belly.

"Maybe this will help you sleep better," I said softly, tucking the blankets around her.

Isabella gave me a grateful smile, her eyes already beginning to droop with fatigue. "Thank you, Cassian. For everything."

I brushed a strand of hair from her face, my heart full as I watched her drift off to sleep. "I'll always be here, Isabella. Whatever you need, I'm here."

That night, as I lay beside her, I couldn't help but reflect on the whirlwind our lives had become. From the scandal that had threatened to tear us apart to the unexpected joys and challenges of pregnancy, we had faced it all together. And through it all, my love for Isabella had only grown stronger, deeper, more certain.

As I listened to the steady rhythm of her breathing, I felt a deep sense of peace settle over me. Yes, there would be more sleepless nights, more moments of uncertainty and fear. But there would also be laughter, love, and the sweet, simple joy of being together.

And in that moment, with Isabella sleeping soundly beside me and our child safe and sound within her, I knew that there was nowhere else I would rather be. Our life together was just beginning, and I couldn't wait to see what the future held.

40

A Greetings from Future Love

The morning light filtered gently through the curtains, casting a soft, golden glow over the room. I watched as Isabella stirred beside me, her face peaceful and serene, a stark contrast to the restless nights we'd both endured recently. Her breathing was steady, her expression relaxed, and for a moment, I simply lay there, taking in the quiet beauty of the scene. It was one of those rare, perfect moments where everything seemed right with the world.

But even in sleep, Isabella was not entirely comfortable. I noticed the subtle shift in her posture, the slight wince as she adjusted herself, no doubt trying to accommodate the weight of our growing child. My heart swelled with a mix of love and concern as I leaned over to brush a gentle kiss against her forehead.

She stirred at the touch, her eyes fluttering open to meet mine. A sleepy smile spread across her face, and I couldn't help but smile back, feeling that familiar rush of affection that had become so much a part of my life.

"Good morning," she whispered, her voice soft and warm.

"Good morning, my love," I replied, my hand moving to rest on the gentle curve of her belly. "How are you feeling?"

She sighed, a mix of contentment and fatigue. "Better, I think. Though I could do without this constant shifting," she added with a wry smile.

I chuckled softly, knowing exactly what she meant. "You've been so strong,

Isabella. I wish I could do more to help."

Her hand reached up to cup my cheek, her eyes filled with love. "You're doing more than enough, Cassian. Just being here, supporting me, loving me... it's everything I need."

Her words warmed my heart, and I leaned in to press a soft kiss to her lips, savoring the simple intimacy of the moment. As I pulled back, I noticed a flicker of discomfort cross her face, and I immediately tensed.

"Are you all right?" I asked, my voice laced with concern.

She nodded, though I could see the effort it took. "Just a little sore. Nothing to worry about."

I frowned slightly, not entirely convinced, but I knew better than to push her. Isabella was nothing if not resilient, and I trusted her to tell me if something was truly wrong.

"Let's get you up and dressed," I suggested, sitting up and offering her my hand. "We've got a busy day ahead, and I want you to be as comfortable as possible."

She took my hand with a grateful smile, allowing me to help her out of bed. As I stood behind her, guiding her toward the wardrobe, I couldn't resist the urge to wrap my arms around her from behind, my hands resting on her belly.

"Cassian," she murmured, leaning back into me, her voice tinged with amusement. "You're getting a little too good at this."

I chuckled, pressing a kiss to her temple. "What can I say? I've found my calling."

We stood like that for a moment, wrapped in each other's arms, the world outside our little bubble fading into the background. There was something incredibly soothing about the way her body fit against mine, the way our child moved within her, a constant reminder of the life we were creating together.

As I helped her dress, carefully selecting a gown that was both comfortable and flattering, I couldn't help but marvel at how far we had come. From the scandal that had threatened to tear us apart to the joy of our wedding day, and now to the everyday moments of married life—we had weathered every storm together, and our love had only grown stronger.

Once she was dressed, I couldn't resist pulling her close again, my arms encircling her waist as I pressed my lips to her neck. "You are the most beautiful woman in the world, Isabella," I whispered against her skin.

She laughed softly, turning in my arms to face me. "You do have a way with words, Cassian. But if you keep this up, we'll never get anything done today."

I grinned, my eyes locking with hers. "Maybe that's the point."

She rolled her eyes playfully but didn't pull away. Instead, she tilted her head up, her lips parting slightly as she leaned in for a kiss.

Just as our lips were about to meet, Isabella suddenly gasped, her hand flying to her belly. I felt her tense in my arms, and a wave of concern surged through me.

"Isabella?" I asked, my voice tight with worry.

She winced, her eyes wide with surprise. "I... I think that was another contraction."

My heart skipped a beat, the playful mood of the moment instantly replaced by a flood of adrenaline. "Another? But it's still too early, isn't it?"

She nodded, biting her lip as she tried to catch her breath. "Yes, but... oh, Cassian, this one feels different."

I quickly guided her to a chair, kneeling beside her as I reached for her hand. "Should we call the midwife? Is it time?"

Isabella's expression was a mix of uncertainty and resolve. "I don't know... it's still too soon, but it feels so strong. Maybe it's just a false alarm, like before."

But even as she said the words, I could see the doubt in her eyes. I knew then that this was different, that we were on the cusp of something monumental.

"I'll send for the midwife," I said, squeezing her hand reassuringly. "We'll figure this out together, whatever happens."

As I moved to call for help, I couldn't help but glance back at Isabella, who was now breathing deeply, trying to manage the pain. In that moment, I was struck by the sheer strength and courage she possessed—qualities that had drawn me to her from the very beginning.

When I returned to her side, the contraction had passed, leaving her a little pale but still composed. "Cassian," she said softly, her voice tinged with a mixture of anxiety and hope. "If this is really happening... if our baby is coming now, I want you to know how much I love you."

Her words hit me like a wave, filling me with an overwhelming sense of love and responsibility. I knelt beside her, taking her face in my hands as I looked into her eyes. "I love you too, Isabella. More than anything in this world. And whatever happens next, we'll face it together. I'll be here with you every step of the way."

She smiled through the tears that had begun to form in her eyes, her hand resting on her belly. "I couldn't ask for a better partner, Cassian. You've given me so much strength."

"And you've given me a reason to be strong," I replied, my voice thick with emotion.

In that moment, all the fears, all the uncertainties, melted away. It didn't matter if the baby was coming early, or if we weren't fully prepared. What mattered was that we were together, ready to face whatever life had in store for us.

As I leaned in to kiss her, the familiar sensation of love and connection flooded through me. But just as our lips met, Isabella gasped again, another contraction rippling through her body.

She laughed breathlessly, her eyes sparkling with both amusement and awe. "Well, I suppose our little one isn't waiting any longer."

I couldn't help but laugh along with her, the tension of the moment easing slightly as we shared that brief, sweet moment of levity. "It seems they've inherited your sense of timing," I teased, brushing a strand of hair from her face.

"Or yours," she shot back, a grin tugging at her lips.

We both knew that the time had come. This was it—the beginning of the next chapter in our lives, a chapter that would bring with it new challenges, new joys, and a love that would only continue to grow.

As we prepared for what was to come, I felt a deep sense of peace settle over me. This was what I had always wanted—a life filled with love, laughter, and a little bit of mischief. And as long as I had Isabella by my side, I knew that no matter what the future held, we would face it together.

With one final kiss, I held her close, feeling the steady beat of her heart against mine, the promise of our future intertwined with every breath we took. And as the contractions grew stronger, signaling the imminent arrival of our child, I knew that we were ready—ready to welcome this new life into the world, and ready to embrace the journey ahead.

41

A Promise for the Future

The hours blurred together, each one marked by the relentless wave of pain that crashed over me. I had known childbirth would be difficult—everyone said so, but nothing could have prepared me for this. The pain was unlike anything I had ever experienced, deep and all-consuming, as if my body were being torn apart from the inside. Each contraction was a vicious reminder of the life I was about to bring into the world, and yet, the baby stubbornly refused to emerge.

I clung to Cassian as if he were my lifeline, his strong arms wrapped around me, grounding me in the midst of the storm. Most husbands waited anxiously outside the room, their nerves frayed as they listened to the cries of their wives, but not Cassian. He had refused to leave my side from the very beginning, insisting on holding me, comforting me, even when the midwife suggested he step back to allow her to work. He wouldn't hear of it, and I was grateful beyond words for his presence.

"Breathe, Isabella," Cassian murmured in my ear, his voice steady and calm despite the fear I could see etched in his eyes. "Just breathe through it, love. I'm right here."

I tried to focus on his words, on the warmth of his hand as it rested on my belly, but the contractions came again, sharper this time, tearing a cry from my throat. My entire body felt like it was on fire, each muscle straining with the effort of trying to bring our child into the world. And yet, after hours of labor, I still hadn't progressed much. The baby wasn't moving down, wasn't coming out as he should.

I could see the worry on the midwife's face, though she tried to hide it behind a mask of professionalism. She had been encouraging, telling me to push, to focus, to breathe, but now, even she seemed uncertain. And I couldn't help but wonder if something was wrong, if perhaps I wasn't strong enough to do this.

"Cassian," I gasped, clutching his arm as another contraction wracked my body. "I can't... I don't know if I can do this."

"You can," he said firmly, his voice laced with determination. "You're the strongest woman I know, Isabella. You can do this. We can do this together."

I buried my face in his chest, trying to draw strength from his unwavering support. The pain was unbearable, searing through my body with each contraction, but worse was the fear gnawing at the edges of my mind—the fear that I wouldn't be able to bring our baby into the world, that something might go wrong, and I would lose both the child and myself.

"Why won't he come out?" I gasped, clutching my swollen belly with both hands, feeling the hard curve of it beneath my fingers. The pressure was immense, unbearable, and yet our baby still seemed so far from being born. "Why is it taking so long, Cassian? Why is my belly still so big?"

Cassian held me tighter, his voice steady and soothing as he whispered into my ear. "You're doing everything right, Isabella. Our baby just needs a little more time. I'm here with you, love. You're not alone."

I could feel the tears of frustration and fear welling up in my eyes, spilling over as I gripped my belly harder, as if I could will our baby to move, to finally make his way into the world. "It hurts so much," I sobbed, my voice trembling with exhaustion. "I don't know if I can do this, Cassian. Why won't he come out? Why is this so hard?"

"I know it hurts, love," he murmured, his hand gently covering mine, pressing softly against my belly. "But you're the strongest woman I know. You've come this far, and I know you can do it. Our baby will be here soon—I promise you that."

Time seemed to stand still as the hours dragged on, each contraction more agonizing than the last. I felt like I was on the edge of breaking, my energy waning as the labor stretched into what felt like an eternity. I could see the worry in the midwife's eyes, her concern clear as she continued to check my progress. The baby wasn't moving down as quickly as he should have been, and every time I pushed, it felt like I was fighting against a wall of resistance.

"I can't, Cassian," I whimpered, my voice barely above a whisper. "I don't have any strength left. Why isn't he moving?"

Cassian pressed his lips to my forehead, his hand never leaving mine as he tried to comfort me. "You're almost there, Isabella," he said softly, his voice thick with emotion. "Our baby is just as strong as you are. He's going to make it, and so are you. We'll get through this together."

The midwife's instructions became more urgent, her concern clear in the way she glanced at Cassian, silently pleading with him to move me to the bed, to allow her to take control. But Cassian refused to leave my side, holding me tightly in his lap, his arms wrapped around me like a shield against the pain.

"Please, my lord," the midwife urged gently, "let me move her to the bed. It'll be easier for her to push."

Cassian looked down at me, his eyes filled with worry and love, but I shook my head weakly, clinging to him as if he were my lifeline. "No," I whispered, my voice trembling. "I need him here with me. Please don't let go, Cassian. I can't do this without you."

He nodded, his jaw set with determination as he tightened his hold on me. "I'm not going anywhere, Isabella. I'll be right here, all the way through."

Another contraction hit me, harder than before, and I cried out, the sound of my own voice startling me with its raw intensity. The pressure in my belly was overwhelming, a crushing weight that seemed impossible to bear. I could feel the baby's head pressing down, but it still felt like he was stuck, like no matter how hard I pushed, he wouldn't come out.

"I'm so tired," I moaned, my head falling back against Cassian's shoulder. "Why won't he come out? I just want it to be over."

Cassian kissed my temple, his voice a soothing balm against the pain. "Just a little more, love. You're almost there. I know it's hard, but you're doing so well. Our baby's almost here—I can feel it."

His words gave me a small spark of hope, a flicker of strength that I clung to as I gathered what little energy I had left. The midwife was speaking to me, her voice calm but insistent as she encouraged me to push again. I took a deep breath, feeling Cassian's arms tighten around me, and pushed with all the strength I had left.

The pain was blinding, but this time, there was a difference. I felt a shift, a movement that sent a surge of relief through me. The baby was finally moving down, the resistance easing as I pushed again, the contractions coming faster, more intense.

"Just a little more, Isabella," he whispered, his voice choked with emotion. "You're doing so well. Our baby's almost here."

I gritted my teeth, gathering every ounce of strength I had left, and pushed with everything in me. The pain reached a crescendo, and for a moment, I thought I might pass out from the intensity of it.

And then, suddenly, the pressure released, and I felt the unmistakable sensation of our baby slipping free. The room was filled with the sound of a newborn's cry, strong and healthy, and I collapsed back against Cassian's chest, my body trembling with exhaustion and relief.

"He's coming," the midwife said, her voice filled with relief. "You're almost there, my lady. Just a few more pushes."

I gritted my teeth, tears streaming down my face as I pushed again, my whole body trembling with the effort. Cassian's voice was in my ear, encouraging me, telling me how proud he was, how close we were to meeting our child.

With one final, agonizing push, I felt the baby's head emerge, followed by the rest of his tiny body, slipping free with a rush of relief so powerful it brought tears to my eyes.

The midwife caught him, quickly wrapping him in a soft blanket, and then handed him to me. I looked down at the tiny, wriggling form in my arms, his cries filling the room, and felt a rush of love so overwhelming it took my breath away.

Cassian's arms tightened around me, his voice choked with emotion as he whispered in my ear. "You did it, Isabella. He's here. Our son is here."

I opened my eyes, blinking through the haze of tears and fatigue, and saw the midwife holding up our baby boy, his tiny body wriggling as he let out another loud cry. She quickly wrapped him in a blanket and placed him in my arms, and I felt a rush of love so powerful it nearly took my breath away.

"He's perfect," I whispered, my voice shaking with emotion as I looked down at our son, his tiny fists waving in the air. "Cassian, look… he's perfect."

Cassian leaned over, his hand trembling as he reached out to touch our baby's soft cheek. "He is," he agreed, his voice filled with awe. "You were amazing, Isabella. I'm so proud of you."

I looked up at him, tears streaming down my face, and saw the love in his eyes, the pride and joy that mirrored my own. We had done this together, brought our son into the world despite all the challenges, and in that moment, I knew that there was nothing we couldn't face as long as we were together.

Cassian leaned down and kissed my forehead, then pressed a gentle kiss to our son's tiny head. "Welcome to the world, little one," he whispered, his voice filled with love. "You have no idea how much we've been waiting for you."

I smiled through my tears, feeling a sense of completeness that I had never known before. Our son was here, safe and healthy, and I was surrounded by the love of the man who had been my rock through it all.

As I held our baby boy close, feeling his warmth and the steady beat of his heart, I knew that this was the beginning of a new chapter for us—a chapter filled with love, joy, and the promise of a future that we would build together, one step at a time.

* * *

Next story about Edmund Fairchild and Beatrice Beatrice Whitford in **The Scandalous Offer for the Duke**

About the Author

Cressida Blythewood is an author of Regency romance novels, renowned for her warm, heartwarming love stories that transport readers to a time of elegance, wit, and enduring passion. With a deep affection for the Regency era, Cressida weaves tales that celebrate the power of love to overcome societal boundaries, misunderstandings, and personal trials, all while ensuring that her characters find their way to a happy ending.

Also by Cressida Blythewood

The Marquess Unexpected Bride

When you set someone up and end up trapped.

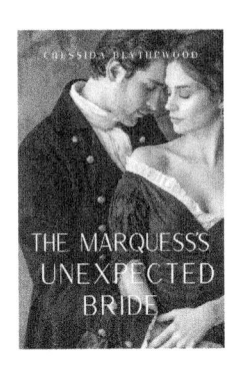

Printed in Great Britain
by Amazon